Dedication

To Margaret Tanner, my very dear friend and fellow author, for her enduring encouragement and friendship.

To Alan, my husband of over forty-nine years, who has been a relentless supporter of my writing and dreams for many years.

To Virginia McKevitt, cover artist and friend, who always creates the most amazing covers for my books.

To You, my wonderful readers, who encourage me to continue writing these stories. It is such a joy knowing so many of you enjoy reading my stories as much as I love writing them for you.

Table of Contents

Matthew's

Redemption

Book One
Winning His Devotion

Cheryl Wright

Matthew's Redemption
(Book One, Winning His Devotion)
This is book two of a multi-author series, and is completely standalone

Copyright 2024 by Cheryl Wright

Small Town Romance Publications
ALL RIGHTS RESERVED

Cover Artist: Black Widow Books

Editing: Sarah Lamb

Chapter One

Somewhere Outside Timberlake Junction, Montana – 1880s

Matthew Horton half lay on the seat in the luxurious Pullman coach. After several hours of walking the corridors of the noisy and rickety train, he was exhausted.

His exhaustion had him paying little attention to his surroundings. Matthew knew it was the total opposite of what he should be doing. His eyes opened abruptly as the stench of strong but expensive perfume wafted into his nostrils. It effectively acted like smelling salts.

He sat up straight, then watched the woman's retreating back as she headed toward the Pullman's dining coach. Matthew supposed he needed to eat as well, but refused to sit with the paying passengers. It didn't pay to get friendly with any of them, otherwise they would use the *friendship* to their advantage.

Heavy footsteps approached him, and Matthew instinctively reached for his guns. "It…it's only me," Henry, the conductor, blurted. "Chef sent me to check if you're ready to eat yet."

Shoving his Colts back into their holsters, he considered the question. "Sure. Might as well while the money bags are out of my hair." Henry rolled his eyes. He was fairly new to the job and Matthew was still teaching Henry what he did and didn't like, and how he expected the young man to behave.

After all, as the railway detective, Matthew overrode anything Henry might take it upon himself to do. "I'll be in my office," he said as Henry hurried back toward the dining car. What he'd give for a comfortable bed. Lack of sleep could get him killed. Especially on the days the railway carried gold. Not that Henry or any of the other railway staff knew that. He didn't need their hysteria, so it was kept it quiet.

He staggered into his private bathroom, still half asleep, and splashed cold water on his red-rimmed eyes. These last minute call-outs were not conducive to his wellbeing. The railway needed protection, and if he didn't do it, who would? The truth was, there were few detectives on the payroll. He'd spoken to the station manager repeatedly about employing more men in this role, but few were willing to put their lives on the line.

Much of that decision was due to not being able to marry. That wasn't exactly true, but what woman wanted to marry a man who spent his days riding the tracks and fighting off bandits? Most would not take the chance.

Mathew shrugged. The big pay packet he received each month stopped him from resigning. Not that he had the time to use that money—he worked far too much to have spare time.

He stared at himself in the mirror. His hair was sticking up every which way. "A bit of water will fix that," he mumbled as he smothered his hair. Reaching for the towel, he barely heard the knock on his office door.

Matthew sighed. As much as he was hungry, he'd hoped for a bit of time before Henry arrived back here with his food. "Enter," he roared from the small bathroom, as he continued fixing his overgrown raven hair back into place.

"Do I know you?" he asked, startled by the pretty stranger standing before him.

She smiled, and his heart pounded. If he didn't know her, he surely wanted to before the end of their shift.

"I'm here for a couple of days. I'm filling in for Martha, who is feeling poorly."

Instead of answering, Matthew grunted and lifted his head slightly. He rarely engaged in conversation if it could be avoided.

The woman stepped forward and placed the tray of food on his desk. The desk he rarely used. His job was to keep the peace and passengers safe. He did not indulge management by filling out the forms they left for him every time he worked. "What did you say your name was?" He quickly caught himself. "In case we see each other again," he added. "I'm…" he didn't get to finish the sentence, as she interrupted him.

"I know who you are—Matthew Horton." She said nothing more, but Matthew knew she'd heard the rumors. Or should that be the rumors that Henry Boswick constantly spread?

He knew what people thought about him. Everyone believed him to be a womanizer. Just because he was a bachelor didn't mean he spent every free moment with women. With the hours he worked, when did they expect Matthew would pursue all these fictitious women? Apart from being unbecoming for a man of his age, it wasn't true.

His job was to protect the passengers of this highly respected railway. Whether he behaved in the manner everyone said he did was irrelevant to his job. Anger built up inside him. Why did people have to share gossip and condemn a person when they did nothing wrong?

The young woman scurried away. No doubt she would keep her distance for the rest of the trip. As he sat down to eat in peace, he realized he didn't know her name. Matthew shrugged. He'd probably never see her again, anyway.

A few minutes later, there was a knock at the door. "Apologies for the interruption, Mr. Horton," Henry said. "Esther forgot your coffee."

Esther. So that was her name. "Thank you, Henry. I assume all is quiet. Are the money bags still eating?" Not that it mattered. He had a job to do and would do it whether or not the passengers were around.

Henry straightened. "Yes, Sir, Mr. Horton. Their dessert and coffee will be served shortly."

Matthew smiled. That meant he had a reprieve for a bit longer. He would finish eating, then do his rounds. So far, so good. Despite that, he was always on alert. Outlaws were clever, some of them at least. They would strike when it was least expected. That's why Matthew always anticipated an attack.

"Thank you, Henry." He had a dislike for the conductor, especially since he didn't get the job on merit, but because the station manager was his uncle. Truth be told, Henry was a weasel. He was only there for his own benefit and didn't care for the passengers. Or the staff. Matthew vowed to sort the young man out if it was the last thing he did.

He stared down at the plate of stew. The railway chef was excellent. His skills were wasted here, but Matthew wasn't complaining. For the price they paid, the Pullman passengers certainly deserved the better class of meal.

Matthew did his rounds once all the passengers had returned, and all their bellies were full. Hopefully, that meant they would keep out of his way. The curtains were pulled back on the windows, which gave him a full view of the area from both sides of the train. His brief was simple—if the train was attacked, it was his job to keep the passengers in his carriage safe. Except Matthew knew the railway hadn't employed enough detectives for each run for months. If they could fill the positions, they would. Having only a few detectives left the railway wide open for attack.

Not that they'd advertised the fact they were short staffed, but people noticed things. Especially those of the unsavory kind. "Afternoon, Mrs. Kilberry," he said, as he passed her in the corridor. Most of the passengers in the Pullman coach were regulars. In Marion Kilberry's case, she traveled to Helena every Friday to shop. Mostly gowns and hats, but other times she bought shoes. Not that it was his concern, but the woman must have an entire room to home her clothes.

"Mr. Horton," she said in her haughty way.

Kneeling on the highly padded seat, Matthew stared out the window again. Still quiet. He turned to see Mrs. Kilberry staring. Matthew came to the conclusion she didn't want him kneeling on the seats. "No bandits," he said, a sly grin on his face, knowing it would annoy her.

She turned away as though she wasn't bothered, but Matthew saw right through her. The look of dread before she turned her head was the result he wanted. Then he felt guilty. Suddenly, she faced him again. "You're not really looking for bandits, are you, Mr. Horton?" Her voice quivered, and he felt even more guilty for scaring her. But only momentarily.

"Do you know what my position here is, Mrs. Kilberry?" he asked sweetly.

She shook her head. Had he scared the railway's best passenger into silence? "I'm a railway detective. My job is to ensure every passenger is safe at all times. I scout the area for outlaws and make sure no one is harassed during their trip."

The woman's eyes opened wide in shock. "Really?" she whispered. "Have you ever had to fight off outlaws?"

Matthew sighed. Did Mrs. Kilberry believe there was some sort of mystery attached to his job? She appeared to be romanticizing his work, but it was far from that. "Never. Which suits me fine." He didn't add things could change in the blink of an eye. "If you'll excuse me, I need to continue on my rounds."

"Of course," she said, and settled herself into her preferred seat. Henry soon brought tea and biscuits, and Mrs. Kilberry seemed settled again.

It couldn't have come too soon for Matthew.

Chapter Two

Esther Walters sat drinking tea in the small area earmarked for staff. Breaks were few and far between in this job, and she snatched them up when the opportunity arose. Mostly, Esther was on her feet the entire time. If it hadn't been for the fact Martha was poorly, she wouldn't even be on this trip.

Like most of her railway colleagues, Esther worked out of Timberlake Junction. Her regular run went from Timberlake Junction, then north to Valley Station. Today she was heading south toward Rivers Edge, Moose Ridge, and a few other smaller stops along the way. For her, it was unchartered territory.

Once she'd finished her tea, Esther washed her mug. It wouldn't do to leave her cup here for someone else to clean. Oh, she knew the kitchen staff would come around later and clean up. That didn't mean they should be treated like slaves. They were all working for a reason—to claim their pay packet at the end of the month.

If there was a choice, it wasn't a job Esther would do. She certainly didn't relish it. Still, she'd done it now for several years. The pay was reasonable, but more importantly, it paid the bills.

Glancing out the window as the train hurried along the tracks, Esther caught a glimpse of… What it was, she didn't know, but something was there. She was certain of it. Despite the train moving at a hurried pace, she saw movement again.

Her heart pounded. What should she do? Esther stood frozen to the spot for about thirty seconds, undecided what her next move should be. If she told the conductor, he would likely laugh at her. Henry was far too immature for his job, and in Esther's opinion, he only had it because his uncle was the manager at the railway station.

Her eyes trained outside, Esther's heart seemed to slow, along with everything around her. A man rode past, but the train moved too fast for her to see much. The door to the room suddenly opened, and she gasped.

"I apologize for startling you, Miss…er, Esther," Matthew Horton told her. Then placed his soiled dishes on the side cupboard. He stared at her. "Are you alright? You look like you've seen a ghost."

Esther lifted a hand and pointed. "A man on a horse," she said, then gasped again. Matthew stepped to her side.

"Out there? You saw a man riding a horse?"

"I…" She was tongue-tied for no other reason than she was scared. Esther had done this job for over a year, and never had her trains been attacked. Was that about to change?

Before she knew it, his hands were on her shoulders, and he gently shook her. "Esther!" he said firmly. "I need you to focus. Tell me exactly what you saw."

She swallowed down her shock and stared into his face. He was staring at her and frowning. "I noticed something move behind some trees. But we were going so fast I thought I might have imagined it." Her hands shook and Esther felt lightheaded at the shock, but knew she needed to continue. "I saw more movement, then after that, a man rode past on a brown horse."

"Is that all?" He studied her closely, and it made Esther nervous.

"He held a gun," she told him, then glanced down at the floor.

"You did good," he said, then hurried to the window. "I need your help. Find Henry and tell him I want all the window coverings closed. All the passengers are to get down low, out of danger."

"The passengers will be terrified," Esther said, knowing it was true.

Matthew stared at her, then said, "Tell them it's a safety drill." Then he turned and left her alone.

Esther didn't know what to think. But she knew she had to act quickly. If they really were being attacked, Matthew would know what to do, and she needed to follow his orders.

She closed the window coverings in the staff room, then hurried to find Henry. He was near useless most of the time, but she hoped he would act accordingly during an emergency. As Esther passed each window, she closed the coverings, hoping she was quick enough.

"What are you doing?" Henry asked, annoyance clear in his voice.

Relaying Matthew's instructions, it was clear Henry did not want to comply. "If you refuse," Esther said, "any injuries or deaths will be on you. First, though, you need to find Mr. Horton and explain you won't be following his orders." She raised her eyebrows to assert her stance.

Suddenly, he was a mass of nerves. "I didn't say I wouldn't do it," he said, his voice quivering. "I simply didn't understand the reasoning." He cricked his neck before speaking again. "Let's get to it then," he said, and hurried toward the main seating area.

Esther followed behind him, continuing with her quest to cover all the windows.

"Ladies and gentlemen," Henry said nervously. "We are having an emergency drill. Please…"

Mrs. Kilberry interrupted him. "A drill? What kind of drill?" she asked, her voice as uncertain as his.

Henry cricked his neck again, then glanced across at Esther. "Mr. Horton has requested this drill, as we haven't had one for a very long time," she said.

The woman didn't look convinced. She opened her mouth to speak, but Esther interrupted her. "Let me help you, Mrs. Kilberry, was it? If you could lie along the length of the seat, that would be perfect." The woman complied, worry all over her face.

Esther was worried too, but she couldn't let the passengers know that. She glanced up to see the detective glancing out windows, moving from one window to another. He put the coverings back in place as he moved around the carriage to watch from various angles. He shrugged his shoulders, and stared her way, and Esther wondered what it meant.

"Thank you for participating in the drill, everyone. Please stay in that position until myself or another staff member lets you know otherwise," Matthew announced.

Esther was still none the wiser, but hurried toward the retreating man as he motioned for her to join him. "I don't see movement, or anyone out there," he whispered. "I'll check the other carriages, and will return shortly."

Then he was gone, and Esther wasn't sure what it all meant. Hopefully, she hadn't sent him on a wild goose chase. Surely it was better to be safe than sorry, but what did it mean for her job?

Chapter Three

As he continued to stare out each of the windows, Matthew felt as though he'd been sent on a fool's errand. Still, it relieved the boredom of walking the corridors endlessly.

Many of the Pullman passengers were long-time travelers. It would do them good to partake in an emergency drill. Having himself and other railway detectives onboard was meant to deter outlaws and other criminals, but Matthew knew firsthand it didn't always work that way. It was rare for any sort of upheaval in his coach, since they attracted a higher class of people. The detectives allocated to the public carriages were not so lucky.

Even during this drill, a fight broke out between two men. One pulled his gun, and Matthew, being the closest to them, intervened. "Break it up," he bellowed, and both men stopped in their tracks. "Any more trouble from you two and you'll be locked up for the rest of the journey. You," he said, pointing to one man and rubbing a hand across his bristled chin, "sit over there. And you," addressing the other one, "Stay right there and don't move."

The two men immediately glared at each other but didn't move from where Matthew placed them.

Thank goodness he spent most of his time in the Pullman carriage. There was no such carry on there. He motioned to the detective allocated to this carriage to monitor the pair. Matthew then continued his perusal out of the windows.

"Everyone needs to get down low," he said. "We are taking part in an emergency drill. I'll be closing the window coverings as part of the drill." He heard the collective gasp of the passengers and quickly reassured them. "It's a drill. Nothing to be alarmed about." At least not yet, he pondered.

Continuing throughout the entire train turned up nothing. Finally, he called off the so-called drill and returned to his own area.

It had Matthew worried. "Thank you, everyone," he announced to the money bags. For once, they'd come through. "The drill was very successful because of your cooperation." Esther glanced toward him, no doubt trying to decipher what his words meant. He motioned her into his office. "Sit down," he said gruffly, not meaning anything by it. The look on her face alerted him Esther believed she was in trouble. He needed to remedy that. His exhaustion was making him cranky, and he knew it. "Tell me again what you saw."

She stiffened and Matthew instinctively knew Esther believed her job was in jeopardy. "You're not in any trouble," he said firmly as he tried to stifle a yawn. He pulled out his pocket watch. "I've hardly slept in over the past days," he said. "Last minute call-out."

"I'm sorry," she said, then reached for his hand. She just as quickly pulled it back. "There were three men altogether. At first I saw what appeared to be the head of a horse—it was at the edge of a clump of trees. Then, further along, another man on a horse, this one in full view. They were still quite a distance away."

Matthew listened intently, writing notes as she spoke. Esther glanced down and noticed his note-taking. "It's so I don't forget anything," he said. "Go on. Tell me about the last man you saw." He rubbed a hand across his roughened chin again. Despite the exhaustion he felt, Matthew was convinced he knew what it was all about.

"He was close to the train. So close I could describe his features." Esther sounded nervous, but everything she told him now fitted with her earlier report.

"Go on," Matthew told her. "Describe him."

Esther's eyebrows lifted, then she leaned forward in her chair. "He was white, with straggly brown hair under his black Stetson. His beard was unkempt, and his clothes appeared ruffled. He held a Colt in his hand." She leaned back as she stopped talking.

Matthew was about to speak when she began again. "Oh, his horse was a lovely brown thoroughbred. He had a diamond on his chest."

It astounded him the amount of detail Esther could provide and he crossed his arms in front of himself. "You're certain about all this?"

"I am absolutely positive," she snapped, then seemed to stare him down.

A smile tugged at his lips, but Matthew kept himself under control. Besides, the situation was far too dire to treat it like a laughing matter.

"Is that all?" she asked, a quiver in her voice. "Are you going to tell the railways to sack me? For wasting your time?"

He studied her. Is that what she thought this was about? "On the contrary," he said, rifling through a drawer in his desk. "Is this the man who was close to the train?" He pushed the wanted poster across the desk to her.

Esther gasped. "That…that's him," she said, her voice unsteady. "What does all this mean?"

"It means they're staking out the train to see if they can attack without being seen. Only your eagle eyes have stopped them in their tracks."

She appeared confused.

"We will double our gun power on the next run and for as long as it takes. We'll be ready for them." He pulled back the poster. "And all because of you."

Matthew stood. "I'll ensure management knows it was because of your diligence we uncovered their plan." He stood as Henry hurried past. "Wait here," he told her, then put his head outside his office door. "Please arrange tea for Esther, and coffee for me. Some cookies or something sweet, too. Good man," he said, without waiting for an answer.

Esther stood as he reentered the office. "I should get back to work," she said, but he motioned for her to sit down again.

Moments later, Henry arrived with a tray filled with the requested beverages and a plateful of delicacies. He didn't seem happy.

"It's not much, but view this as a small reward for your due diligence," Matthew told her as Henry left the office. "And for keeping the passengers calm. You are a valued member of this railway."

He wondered if Esther would be interested in changing to this route instead of her usual route. She was definitely an asset.

Esther glanced across at him, curiosity written all over her face. After apparently being informed of his reputation when she first arrived, perhaps Esther was now seeing him in a different light. Matthew hoped so. Why people had to spread unfounded rumors, he didn't know. He was a hardworking man who was far from womanizing. His biggest vice was working far more than he should.

"I really should go," Esther protested. "I have work to do."

Matthew studied her. He didn't want to pull rank, but he could easily do so. "You won't get in any trouble." He leaned forward and spoke again. "I am in charge of this carriage. What I say goes."

Her nod was almost unperceivable, but it was there. Picking up his coffee, he watched her over his mug. "I don't like to drink alone—or eat," he said, then reached for one of the mixed pastries on the tray. Suddenly, he pulled back. Where were his manners? "Ladies first," he said, and watched as her shaking hand reached out.

He gently grasped her tiny wrist. A zing went up his arm, and he knew the reason. "No need to be frightened," he said. "I'm not going to hurt you." Matthew heard her sigh, then pulled his hand away. He wished he hadn't. Touching her did something to him. Esther Walters was getting to him.

Thankfully, he wouldn't see her again beyond the next couple of days. When Martha was fully recovered, she would return. As much as Esther had uncovered a possible ambush, it would not pay to have her close.

He studied Esther as she enjoyed her reward. It was best she wasn't staying. He wasn't sure his heart couldn't take it.

Chapter Four

Esther knew she should run, leave Matthew's office right this second. His touch did strange things to her. Oh, she knew the rumors—he was a notorious womanizer. One thing she was certain about, she would not become another notch on his belt.

"I really must go," she said slightly above a whisper.

He frowned. "Wait here," he demanded, then stepped outside his office, closing the door behind him. At least there were glass panels on the doors and everyone could see inside. Otherwise tongues would wag and where would she be then?

Moments later, she noticed Henry in conversation with Matthew. Henry glanced toward her, then back to Matthew. He nodded, then left.

She glanced away in case Matthew saw her watching. The door opened abruptly and alarmed her. "Sorry," he said. "I didn't mean to startle you. I told Henry you would be here with me for a while, and you wouldn't be available until later."

It took all her effort not to complain. He'd already explained her job was safe, but what would her coworkers think? She was not one to slack; Esther prided herself on being a hard worker. The other staff might not know her on this train route, but she didn't want to earn a poor reputation on her first day here.

"You're not happy?" he asked, a frown marring his face. "I thought you'd be ecstatic."

It took all her effort not to roll her eyes. "I… Don't think I'm not grateful," she said, "because I am." Esther straightened in her chair. "This is my first day on this line. I don't want anyone to think I'm trying to get out of work."

He frowned again, but didn't say a word. She picked up her cup of tea and sipped it. Anything to distract from the conversation and the man sitting opposite her.

"We both know that's not true," he said. "You need to stop worrying about gossip and listening to rumors." His last words were firm. Esther knew exactly what he meant. He was referring to the gossip about his being a womanizer.

She gulped down the last of her tea, then stood. "I need to go," she said firmly. "The kitchen will be preparing for the dinner service. They need my help."

Before he could respond, she hurried out of his office. He seemed like a good man, and he was certainly looking out for her. Did Matthew have his eye on her as a conquest? She hoped not. When and if she fell for a man, it would be someone solid. A man who did not pluck women like they were chicken feathers. She wanted a man who was interested in her for who she was, not what she could give to him.

Esther shook her head as she almost reached the kitchen. She leaned against the corridor wall, trying to take it all in. He hadn't told her either way, but she would keep that information about a potential train robbery to herself. If word got around, it might warn the robbers.

She dreaded being on the train when they hit. Hopefully, she would be back on her own line when it happened. It sounded awful, she admitted, but having it happen without warning was totally different from knowing something horrific was about to hit. Her heart pounded at the thought.

A few days had passed and Esther was still filling in for Martha. She must be quite ill, Esther decided. She hoped the woman recovered completely and was back at work soon.

The moment the thought entered her mind, Esther knew she was being selfish. She'd settled into her temporary position on this route, and nothing untoward had happened. She hoped that meant Matthew Horton was wrong. What those men were up to, she did not know, but if there were to be a robbery, wouldn't it have happened by now?

The railway had supplied extra manpower, but for what? They were clearly only guns for hire, and not professional detectives like Matthew Horton and the other detectives employed by the railway.

Esther knew from experience they would soon tire of paying for additional staff when they deemed it unnecessary. After all, they were a business, and businesses needed to make money. Spending the least amount possible was their aim.

Glancing up, Esther noticed Henry heading toward her, a determined look on his face. "Esther," he said hurriedly. "Mrs. Kilberry would like tea and cake. Now!"

Forcing herself not to react negatively at Henry's sudden burst of power, she turned and hurried into the kitchen. Making up a tray for the demanding woman took mere minutes, and she headed out. Mrs. Kilberry was demanding, but not rude, like some travelers. Especially those in the public section.

She filled a pot with tea, a small jug with milk, then added a sugar bowl on the side. Lemon cake was today's delicacy, and she placed two slices on a small plate for Mrs. Kilberry, then left the small kitchen used for just this purpose.

As a regular passenger, Mrs. Kilberry received special treatment.

She glanced about the Pullman coach upon entering, but couldn't immediately see the elderly woman. Until she turned. She was wearing a new hat, which she more than likely picked up on her visit.

"Ah, Esther," Mrs. Kilberry said. "Thank you, my dear. I've been visiting my sister, and now I'm quite parched." It was clear to Esther the woman was lonely, and familiar faces on the railway filled a gap not realized elsewhere. "I do hope you'll be staying with us. I know you're filling in for Martha, but you are far more competent than she is."

The older woman's words shocked Esther. She didn't know Martha at all, but hearing those words from a passenger was astonishing. Especially when she didn't want to be here, knowing there could be a robbery at any moment.

"Thank you, Mrs. Kilberry," was all she said before turning away.

"I know the owner. I'll speak with him." Her words trailed off as Esther left.

A shiver went down Esther's spine and her heart pounded. She didn't want to be on this line permanently. She'd worked for the railway long enough to learn most of the Pullman travelers were self-centered in their endeavors. If Mrs. Kilberry wanted her there, it was for the woman's own benefit, not Esther's. She would surely get nothing out of it.

She also didn't want to be caught up in a robbery. It was always a possibility when the railway line carried gold. Despite not telling their staff, they all knew it happened. Rumors abounded around the practice. Trains were less likely to be robbed than stagecoaches, which had become easy prey.

Empty tray in her hand, she hurried back to the kitchen, certain Henry would have another assignment for her. He always did.

Chapter Five

Matthew took his time strolling the length and breadth of the Pullman coach. Stopping to chat here and there with passengers, all the while glancing out the windows. Little did they know of the threat to their safety, but it wasn't something he could share.

As he rounded the corner, he collided with something hard. Matthew was almost knocked off his feet, but glancing down he saw the reason for the accident.

Esther Walters.

She was flat on her back, a tray balancing on her stomach—only because she held on to it for dear life. "Miss Walters, Esther, are you alright?" he asked as he leaned down to help the woman to her feet.

"I…I apologize," she stammered. "I obviously wasn't looking where I was going."

He frowned. "It takes two," he told her. "Apparently I wasn't either." His hands reached out to her, but she continued to clutch onto the tray. "I'll take that," he said firmly, and moved the tray to the side. The moment his hands touched hers, a shiver went through him. He let go of her hands. To his horror, she fell back again. Matthew moved quickly to save her from hitting the floor.

Again.

He stared down at the woman in his arms. She was petrified, and he didn't doubt it was his fault. "I apologize. I don't normally drop women." He grinned then and hoped it reassured her somewhat.

It was at that very moment, Henry rounded the corner and almost collided with the pair. He looked them up and down for mere seconds, then demanded to know what was going on.

"Miss Walters and I collided. I was helping her to her feet." Henry looked unimpressed. Matthew was fuming. He did not answer to this little weasel. "She needs to rest now, since she hit her head on the hard floor."

"I…" Esther began to protest, but Matthew interrupted.

"Miss Walters can sit in my office until she feels better." His words were firm. Henry might try to rule the roost, but Matthew had the final say. "Please arrange a tray with tea for Miss Walters, and coffee for me. A plate of cookies as well, thanks."

He handed the tray to Henry. The man simply stared at it.

He didn't wait for any response, and immediately led Esther to his office. "We can't have you wandering about if you have a head injury," he said, and winked as he helped her into a chair. Matthew then sat on the other side of the desk.

"Henry was fuming," she whispered. "He doesn't enjoy being told what to do."

"That's his problem," Matthew told her. "Henry is in charge of *his* staff. I am in charge of *all* the staff on this train. I'm the Chief Railway Detective." He leaned a little closer across the desk that separated them. "Henry doesn't like it," he whispered.

That made her smile. Chuckle even. He liked when she smiled, and his heart did funny things. Matthew didn't like that. There was only room for one thing in his life, and that was his job.

"Ah, Henry," Matthew said when the door opened moments later. "Thank you. I'm sure this will help Miss Walters."

Henry stared at him momentarily, then frowned. He opened his mouth to say something, but apparently thought the better of it as he slammed it shut again. He then turned and hurried out of Matthew's office.

"How is your head?" he asked the moment Henry closed the door.

"There is nothing wrong with my head." She studied him then. "You made that up!" This time, she sounded flabbergasted.

"You must be worse than I thought," Matthew told her. "I clearly remember hearing your head hit the floor." He grinned at her then. No such thing had occurred, but he wasn't taking any chances. If she banged her head on that hard floor, it could have serious repercussions. "Now drink up your tea."

"Do you know when Martha is due to return to work?" Esther asked. She seemed concerned about the woman. "I'm concerned for two reasons," she said, and Matthew studied her but didn't interrupt. "First, if I was called in to take her place for perhaps a week, she must be quite ill." She glanced down into her teacup before answering again. "Second, Mrs. Kilberry said she plans to speak to the owner about having me transferred to this line." Esther scowled, making it clear she didn't agree with the other woman's request.

"You don't want to work here permanently?" He scrutinized her, trying to work out why she hated being on this line so much.

She took another sip of her tea. "It's not that I don't like it here. Although Henry is hard to take. It's…" Esther placed her teacup in its saucer. "Passengers shouldn't get to dictate who works for the railway."

She was right, of course she was. "Mrs. Kilberry?" he asked, knowing it would be her. Not only was she rich, she was influential and knew it.

Esther nodded. "I don't want to put another worker out of a job, either."

Matthew stiffened. "That won't happen. Worse case scenario, the two of you could swap lines."

"What if I don't want to do that?" She closed her eyes momentarily, then stared into his face. "There could be a train robbery," she whispered.

Matthew leaned across and covered her hand. "That could happen no matter the line. It's still a possibility, but looking less likely by the day." He glanced out the window as he said the words. Nothing but trees, scrub, and dust surrounded them.

Dust!

Matthew stood and ran to the window. "Get down. No!" he yelled, changing his mind. "Go to Henry. Tell him we're being attacked. He'll know what to do." Her face was filled with horror, but he couldn't worry about that now. "Come straight back here once you've told Henry. I need your help with the passengers."

His heart pounded, but Matthew had to ignore it. He had more important things to worry about. Passengers to protect, and he had to get the word out to the hired guns who had been having a free ride all this time. Thanks to Esther, they were prepared for the worst, but that didn't mean they'd get through unscathed. He had the scars from previous attacks to prove it.

Reaching for the rifle he kept stored in his office, Matthew filled it with bullets, then filled his pockets with spares. He hurried into the Pullman coach and instructed the passengers to lie down. Panic filled the room, but thankfully, Esther arrived and restored calm.

She glared at him. He could have been more tactful, but he didn't have time for that.

Matthew ran to the windows and closed the coverings to stop the attackers from seeing inside. He could slide a rifle barrel behind a closed covering and still see outside, but the robbers couldn't see them. He barked out orders to the hired guns who did what they were told. Studying the landscape, he noticed the thoroughbred, the one with the diamond on its chest, which Esther had seen previously. It was running alongside the train—riderless.

Matthew swore under his breath. It likely meant the rider was on the train. That was the last thing they needed.

 Chapter Six

This was it. The very thing Esther had been trying to avoid, and now she was stuck right in the thick of it.

At least she could take comfort in the fact the detectives were ready for the robbery. If she hadn't been so eagle-eyed, as Matthew had called it, they would likely be in a far worse position right now.

"I feel faint," Mrs. Kilberry told her as Esther tried to get the woman to lie down.

"Totally understandable," she told the passenger. "I'll take you to your room and you can rest there. You'll be safe in your room."

The older woman nodded. The feather on her hat appeared almost comical. But this was no laughing matter, and Esther knew it. She helped Mrs. Kilberry to her feet, then led her to her room. Once inside, she helped her out of her very expensive shoes, and with the removal of the equally expensive hat. "Your new hat is beautiful," Esther said, trying to calm the woman further. The sooner she had her calm and resting, the sooner she could get back to the other passengers. "Let me cover you with this spare blanket," she said, reaching into the cupboard. Once the woman was comfortable, she left the room, locking the door behind her.

Once outside, Esther released a sigh of relief. Then she heard it. The popping sound that went along with gun shots. She knew once she got closer the noise would be ear shattering, but from here, it sounded like muffled popping noises.

Her heart pounded until she could barely hear anything around her. Was Matthew alright? Had he been shot? She should never have left the main area to bring Mrs. Kilberry here. Only she knew she'd done the right thing—the woman was panicked and would have set off the other passengers, had she not isolated her.

She hurried back to the lounge area of the Pullman coach. Suddenly, it was quiet. The shooting had stopped, but Matthew was nowhere to be seen. Panic hit her. Only Esther had no time for panic. Her one and only job was to keep the passengers calm. It was all part of her training, but today was the first time she'd had to use it.

"Esther," one passenger called. "It is over? Can we sit up again?" The woman sounded downright distraught, and Esther fully understood.

"Not yet, Mrs. Salsbury. We have to wait for the all-clear from Matthew Horton." Assuming he was unharmed. Esther swallowed. When did she start caring about what happened to the railway detective? The sooner they transferred her back to her own line, the better.

She spun around at shuffling behind her. The man on the wanted poster was being shoved along the corridor by Matthew. He wore handcuffs.

"The rest are all but gone, boss," one of the hired guns said. Esther was ecstatic, but knew she couldn't celebrate yet. Nor could she give the passengers the all-clear without the detective's say so.

"Take another man with you, and double check the roof. I need to lock this low-life up."

Lock him up? Where did Matthew intend to do that?

"Get moving," he said, shoving the man in the back again, heading toward his office. Esther followed. She needed to find out what he wanted her to do about the passengers.

To her surprise, there was a hidden panel behind his desk, and inside was a room with a small jail cell. At first she gasped, and then she smiled. Ingenious. As far as she was aware, this didn't exist on her regular line. But then again, she didn't know it existed on this one.

After locking the man up and closing the hidden panel again, Matthew turned to her. "You need me?" His words were hurried.

"What should I do with the passengers? Is the danger over now?" She heard the pleading in her own voice, but hoped he didn't.

He frowned. "Are you alright?"

"As good as can be expected. I thought, with the shooting stopped…" She stared at him, waiting for an answer.

"Not yet," he said, then hurried away.

Esther's heart sank. This was the one thing she hoped to avoid. But working for the railways, it was inevitable, she supposed.

She hurried back to the passengers. Glancing around at the terrified faces, she made a decision. "I'll fetch tea, shall I?" she asked, and was greeted with far more affirmatives than she could count. "I'll be right back," she said, then hurried toward the kitchen.

Passengers huddled around the trolley full of several pots of tea, milk, sugar, and cookies. As quickly as she poured the tea, it disappeared. So did the cookies. The trolley was soon depleted, and she headed back to the kitchen to refill it. While there, she realized the frivolity of her actions, especially in a time of such uncertainty. Still, Esther did what she had to do—and it was keeping the passengers calm. Wasn't that what she'd been charged with doing?

The moment she entered the Pullman coach again, she was surrounded. Almost to the point she couldn't breathe. Esther knew it was panic making her feel that way, but she couldn't, and wouldn't let the passengers see her fear.

Soon everyone had a cup of tea and cookies, and were sitting calmly, awaiting further instructions. She fetched Mrs. Kilberry from her room and set her up with refreshments as well.

What Esther wouldn't do for a hot cup of tea right now. But that's not what she was being paid to do. She spun around and headed back to the kitchen where she would empty the trolley and clean it, ready for the next time it was needed.

In front of her stood the detective. Matthew. He stood tall and strong, but she could see he was tired. There were lines on his forehead she couldn't recall seeing before, and instead of that grin she loved so much, his lips were in a tight line. His usually tidy hair was messed up, and she wanted nothing more than to run her fingers through it and put each strand back in place.

Esther stiffened. She was not falling for the womanizer standing in front of her. She would not!

"Are you alright?" he asked quietly, then stepped toward her.

She nodded, afraid if she opened her mouth, her emotions might take on a life of their own. As if he knew how she was feeling, Matthew opened his arms to her. Esther refused to be comforted by this man. The man with a reputation for picking up women and throwing them to the wolves when he was done with them.

Her thoughts didn't deter her, and he enveloped her before she could stop him. "It's over," he whispered. "Thanks to you, they didn't get the gold, and we caught the ringleader."

A tear slid down her face in relief. Esther wiped it away. All of a sudden, there was a ruckus behind them. "What are you doing?" Henry demanded, then crossed his arms in front of himself.

"None of your business," Matthew said, glaring at the conductor. "Turn around and go back to where you came from."

"Harrumph!" she heard Henry say, and it took all her effort not to laugh. Only Esther knew if she laughed, she would surely fall into a sobbing heap.

She glanced up at Matthew. He was grinning. "I can't stand that weasel," he said, and soon they were both laughing.

Chapter Seven

Matthew glanced down at the woman in his arms. He knew he shouldn't, but he was enjoying holding her for the second time today. Fighting against his own feelings, he knew Henry was right. He shouldn't be holding Esther, another employee, this way. Only she needed it.

Truth be told, he did too. And she didn't complain. Nor did she push him away, so where was the harm?

His heart fluttered as he continued to hold her. They were both adults, and he was convinced Esther wanted him to hold her close, as much as he wanted to. "Esther," he whispered. She glanced up and stared at him. "Are you alright? As much as I hate to admit it, that little weasel is right."

She pushed back from him. Matthew forced his arms to drop to his sides. That was not where he wanted them to be. "I… I am now," she whispered. "I apologize. My emotions got the better of me."

He nodded, and without warning, she hurried in the opposite direction to where she'd originally been heading. The trolley stood forlornly next to him, and

Matthew smiled as he watched her retreat. He knew how she felt. He was feeling it too, but he'd convinced himself it was nothing more than the result of being in a stressful situation together.

Glancing down at the trolley, he began to roll it back to the kitchen. When he arrived there, Henry was talking to another worker. Or should that be barking orders? Matthew pushed the trolley into the kitchen. "There you are Henry," he said. "This trolley needs to be cleaned."

"But I…"

He didn't wait for the weasel's answer. Matthew already knew he would protest, but it was too darned bad. Funny thing, he didn't see Henry anywhere while the attack was going on. Esther spent the entire time either in the Pullman coach calming passengers, or bringing them refreshments, no doubt to the same end.

She had a lot of sass, and he appreciated that. Too bad she would transfer away once Martha was back. Martha was fine, but was an older woman and didn't have the energy, or the forethought Esther had. She couldn't think for herself, which was a pity, but Henry would love that. He adored barking out orders. The man resented Matthew's refusal to be dictated to, but frequently gave orders to Henry.

Having the station master as his uncle meant Henry believed he was immune to repercussions. He wasn't.

Matthew made his way back to the Pullman coach. Esther was checking each of the passengers and ensuring they had fully recovered from their ordeal. Mrs. Kilberry, he noticed, seemed particularly rattled. She lived a sheltered life, from what Matthew had seen. An ordeal like this would not be part of her normal life. She would likely see it as a nightmare.

He walked over and sat beside her. "How are you doing, Mrs. Kilberry?" he asked gently. "I believe Esther has been looking after everyone."

"It was scary, Mr. Horton," she said, a quiver in her voice. "But that Esther, she's got what it takes. You need to push for her to stay."

And if I don't, you surely will, he thought, knowing it was true. "I'm afraid the station manager is in charge of all that. Besides, Esther may not want to stay on this line."

Mrs. Kilberry waved a hand in front of herself. "What utter rubbish! I've seen the way she looks at you." She raised her eyebrows then. "You look at her in the same way."

"Nonsense!" Matthew sputtered. "We barely know each other."

A sly smile crossed her lips. "I know what I see. Besides, she's a good worker. Better than that Martha. I hope she never comes back." She turned away then. Mrs. Kilberry had said her piece, and that was the end of the conversation.

Matthew took the hint and stood. He wandered around the carriage, ensuring everyone had recovered, opening the window coverings as he did so. It was always good to see what was going on outside, especially after an ordeal such as the one they'd already endured.

When all the windows were exposed again, Matthew headed toward his office. As he opened the door, banging greeted him. *What now?* His prisoner was going to be a problem. It was now becoming clear.

"What is your problem, Hayes?" he said, and the man recoiled. He clearly believed Matthew didn't know who he was. The wanted poster he showed to Esther had all the information he needed—Levi Hayes was head of the Renegade Gang, a bunch of misfits who spent most of their time robbing trains. They also hit banks in between the gold runs.

"I'm hungry," he said, and Matthew knew it had nothing to do with being hungry. He simply wanted to make trouble and was likely planning an escape. If he thought his men were going to save him, he'd be wrong. They shot two dead, and three others were seriously injured. Levi Hayes was on his own.

"I'll see what I can do." Matthew turned to leave and flinched at the outlaw's next words.

"Make sure you send that pretty little waitress with my food."

Slamming the hidden door behind him, Matthew cursed under his breath. Everyone would have been better off if a bullet had finished the vile man off. Instead, the railways had to feed him until they handed him over to the authorities. One thing the detective knew for sure, Esther was not going anywhere near that dreadful creature.

He strode to the kitchen and accosted Henry. "I need a plate of food for the prisoner. I guess we better supply a drink, too. Nothing hot. Water maybe—otherwise he's likely to weaponize it."

"Sure, boss," Henry said with a snicker.

Matthew stared him down. He stood over the far shorter man by at least a foot. "You got something to say, Boswick? If so, say it now. Otherwise, shut your filthy mouth." He leaned over the conductor, knowing full well his actions came across as menacing. He'd had more than enough of the weasel for one day.

"N…no, Sir, Mr. Horton," Henry said. "I'll get right on it."

"And Henry, bring it yourself. I won't have any of the women put in danger." Henry's eyes opened wide in fear. Matthew enjoyed watching the awful man shudder, but put him out of his misery. "You'll be fine. I don't want the women to worry, that's all."

Matthew felt a modicum of guilt, but Henry needed to be put in his place. He was power hungry and acted like a dictator to the staff under him. In his gut, Matthew was certain Henry Boswick was the one spreading unfounded and untrue rumors about him, but so far had no proof.

There were far more qualified people available to fill the conductor's shoes, and if he had his way, Matthew would rid the railway of the fool they had there now. Unfortunately, with his uncle as station manager, it was highly unlikely to happen.

Heck, Esther was better suited to the position than Henry would ever be. His heart fluttered at the thought of the pretty little waitress, as Hayes had called her. He might be revolting, but the man was right. Except her beauty went far deeper than what could be seen on the surface. She was cool headed, she was attentive, and Esther was far more intelligent than most people gave her credit for.

He shook his head, trying to clear all thought of Esther Walters. He had a job to do, and it didn't include her. Not now, anyway.

Pulling the door open in a hurry, he plopped down into the chair at his desk. What a day it had been. Actually, what a week. If Esther hadn't seen those men checking out the train, things could have turned out far worse today.

The best part was, not even one of the railway staff were injured. No passengers were harmed. It all made Matthew feel very happy.

There was a tap at the door, then Esther entered, holding a tray of food. "For the prisoner," she said quietly.

Matthew was fuming. "I told Boswick to bring it himself," he said, his lips pulled in a tight line.

"Henry said you requested me." Now she looked deflated.

"For your safety," he added. He heard himself grunt, then Esther's lips curled in a smile. "I'll take it. I won't have you go anywhere near that animal."

He took the tray from her hands, then pushed the hidden door open with his feet. "Sit on the bed," he demanded, then watched as Hayes reluctantly retreated to the back of the cell. Matthew pushed the tray under the door, then left the man alone again.

This trip couldn't finish quick enough for his liking. At the next stop, they'd rid themselves of the outlaw, and things would hopefully go back to normal. He pulled out his pocket watch. "Another hour until we hit Willow's Bend. We'll offload him then."

Esther nodded, then quickly retreated. She seemed to avoid him since… His mind wandered back to the moment he held her in his arms. It was pure bliss. Matthew was sure she felt it, too. He would have stayed there forever too, except Henry Boswick interrupted them.

His fury mounting again, Matthew decided it was time to walk it all off. Why he let the conductor get under his skin, Matthew didn't know. Perhaps it was the fact he'd been elevated to that position by family connections. He wasn't certain, but what he was sure of was the fact the weasel did not know what he was doing. It was pure luck they'd gotten through the attack virtually unscathed. He was certain it was due more to Esther's actions than Henry's.

As he pounded the corridors, the aroma of freshly cooked food reached him. Matthew breathed deeply. It enticed him to continue in that direction, when normally he would have turned back. When he reached the door to the kitchen, he was sorely tempted to enter. Suddenly, several waitresses streamed out. Esther was one of them. His heart fluttered just seeing her there.

He'd seen the passengers heading toward the dining room earlier. How could he forget it was time for luncheon? Easy—he'd had one heck of a morning, that's how. Instead of heading back to his empty office or the equally empty lounge in the Pullman coach, he followed the waitresses. He wasn't doing that because of Esther. Definitely not. Besides, it was his job to ensure passenger safety.

If he told himself enough times, he might believe it.

Matthew pushed open the door to the dining room, which was packed with passengers. He glanced across and mentally counted the number of people there. He frowned. Someone was missing. Before he could work out who it was, Esther hurried up to him. "Mrs. Eastlake hasn't arrived for luncheon," she said. "I can't leave now, but wondered if you could check?"

"I've been trying to work out who was absent," he said. "I'll check on her now."

Hurrying down the corridor, he reached the Pullman coach in record time. Most of the passengers who used the Pullman coach were either elderly or rich. The majority were both. Mrs. Eastlake fell into that category. If she'd had a fall, who knew what awaited him?

"Mrs. Eastlake?" Matthew called the moment he entered the exclusive carriage. He stopped and listened. Nothing. "Mrs. Eastlake? Are you here?" He moved further into the carriage. She was nowhere to be found. Matthew pulled the passenger list from his pocket. Perhaps she'd fallen asleep in her room. He snatched up the master key from his belt. Only he and Boswick had a copy, and they rarely had to use it.

This was one time he wouldn't hesitate. Unlocking the door, he continued to call her name, but there was still no response. Once the door was finally open, he discovered the elderly woman lying on the floor. Her body was twisted in a most unnatural way.

"Oh, Mr. Horton," she said weakly. "I thought I was doomed to die in here."

He was no doctor, but Matthew was convinced she had broken a bone. "Help is here, Mrs. Eastlake. Let me put a pillow under your head." After doing so, he reached for the spare blanket and covered her. "I'm afraid I can't move you, but I will get help."

He stood to go, but the elderly woman reached for his hand. "Thank you. You're an angel, despite what people say about you."

Matthew squeezed her hand. "I'll be back shortly," he said, reluctantly leaving her there by herself. Then hurried to the dining room. "Is there a doctor here? Or a nurse?" he called. He glanced over the tables, hoping to find at least one person to help. No one moved.

Suddenly, a hand shot up. "I'm a doctor," the man said.

Matthew had seen him but had no contact before now. "Thank you," he said, shaking the doctor's hand. "One of the elderly passengers has fallen. I think she may have broken her hip," he explained.

"Did you move her?" the man asked, then introduced himself as Doctor Francis Dunne.

"Not at all," Matthew said. "I've made Mrs. Eastlake comfortable with a pillow and blanket, but that's all."

"Good man," Doctor Dunne said, and Matthew was relieved. He certainly meant no harm to the woman.

They hurried down the corridor until they came to Mrs. Eastlake's room. He gently opened the door. "It's Matthew Horton," he said gently. "I have Doctor Francis Dunne with me." He opened the door wider to let the doctor enter ahead of him.

"My dear lady," the doctor said. "What have you done to yourself?" It was clearly rhetorical, and he didn't wait for an answer. Instead, the doctor removed the blanket and studied the unnatural way her limbs lay. "Are you in pain, Mrs. Eastlake?" he asked as he squatted down and studied her.

Matthew stood back out of the way and watched as the doctor examined his patient. He checked her pulse, then gently ran his hands over her suspect hip and down the corresponding leg. He then covered her up again. "We will be back momentarily," he told his patient, then ushered Matthew out of the room.

"Thankfully," he said when they were alone, "it is not a broken hip. A patient of this age likely wouldn't survive such an injury." He put a finger to his chin, as though deep in thought. "I believe Mrs. Eastlake has broken her femur. Her thigh bone," he added for clarity. "In which case it is safe to move her, but not until I can splint it." He explained what supplies he needed to do that, then hurried to his own room to retrieve his medical bag.

Returning to Mrs. Eastlake's room, Matthew explained to the passenger what was about to occur. "Once the doctor returns, everything will be sorted," he said, not convinced there would be a good outcome. Off the top of his head, Matthew believed Mrs. Eastlake would have to be close to eighty now. Mid seventies, at least.

The door slowly opened, and it surprised him to see Esther peeking around the door. She didn't say a word, but Matthew filled her in. "You poor dear," Esther said, then moved inside and held the woman's hand.

Every time he saw Esther, he was shown a different layer of her compassion. She could have easily gone off and had a break now, but instead, she needed to reassure herself the passenger was safe.

"I'm going to need two sturdy splints," the doctor said, rubbing his chin. "Preferably wooden. Oh, and nothing sharp."

Matthew stared at him. He couldn't think of anything except a ruler, and he only had one of those.

"I could get some wooden spoons from the kitchen," Esther offered.

"Perfect," Doctor Dunne told her. "Please hurry."

As Esther left the room, Doctor Dunne administered laudanum. "This will dull the pain. Once your leg is splinted, Mr. Horton and I will move you to the bed. You'll be far more comfortable there. I'm afraid this is going to result in a hospital stay."

"I understand, Doctor," Mrs. Eastlake said. It was one of the few times she'd spoken since Matthew had found her injured.

In what seemed record time, Esther returned with the wooden spoons. She handed them over to the doctor, then resumed her position next to the patient, holding her hand and reassuring her.

"Mr. Horton, I need you to hold these in place once I set the bones, if you don't mind." He pulled the bones into place, with barely a whimper from Mrs. Eastlake, who was dosed up with laudanum. Using the wooden spoons as temporary splints, he then bandaged the leg in place.

It amazed Matthew what the doctor did without the proper tools. "We need to lift Mrs. Eastlake up onto the bed," he said, and showed Matthew exactly what needed to be done to ensure no further damage.

Esther pulled back the covers, and put the pillow in place, then the men carefully and gently lifted the unconscious patient onto the bed. "Are you able to stay with her until we reach Helena?" Doctor Dunne asked.

Matthew heard Esther's intake of breath. "She can stay," he said. "I'll make the arrangements." He turned to the doctor then and shook the man's hand. "Thank you, Doctor Dunne. I don't know what we would have done without you."

The doctor waved Matthew's words aside. "It was nothing. We need to make arrangements at the next station for an ambulance to be waiting when we arrive in Helena."

"Consider it done," Matthew said, then followed the doctor out of the room. "I can't thank you enough," he said. "We've had nothing like this happen before. Now I need to speak to Esther's supervisor."

The men parted company, and Matthew pondered the day's events. He never wanted to have the passengers put through all that angst again.

Chapter Eight

Esther sat on the chair beside Mrs. Eastlake's bed. She could only imagine Henry's reaction when he found out she would not be under his supervision for the rest of the trip. All the way to Helena.

It made sense to wait until then to transfer the woman to the hospital. Helena had the largest hospital in the area. For all she knew, Doctor Dunne likely worked out of there.

There was a light tap on the door, then Matthew tucked his head around the corner. Esther's heart fluttered. "I've brought a tray of tea and cake for you," he whispered. "Doctor Dunne said it would be an hour or more before Mrs. Eastlake wakes up."

He entered the room and placed the tray on the bedside table. "I'll check in later in case you need a break," he said, his voice still low.

"Thank you," Esther whispered back. "How is Henry taking the news?"

Matthew grinned. "You know Henry, but he has no choice. Your help is needed here. I'll leave you in peace." He left as quickly as he arrived.

Esther was trying to attribute this version of Matthew Horton with the one portrayed in the rumors. She simply couldn't see it. How could a man with his level of empathy at work be totally different away from his job?

She poured herself a cup of tea. Matthew was the epitome of kindness. He helped others all the time. She'd seen it time and time again since she'd arrived on this line, and now she questioned the rumors.

As she sipped her tea, which was definitely appreciated, Esther thought back to when she'd arrived. She had little contact with anyone except Henry. And she recalled he was the one to spread the gossip. *Keep away from Matthew Horton, the railway detective. He is a known womanizer.*

Continuing to sip her tea, although she was fuming, Esther was glad she was locked in here, away from the unpleasant man. She was beginning to see Henry Boswick was a sad, entitled shell of a man. It was clear now why Matthew didn't like him. Until she found out his uncle was the station manager, she couldn't understand how Henry had secured the position.

He truly didn't deserve it.

Esther shook her head. She needed to stop thinking about Henry Boswick, and concentrate on the job at hand. Not that it was difficult. She was enjoying the pot of tea Matthew had brought to her, not to mention the orange cake. One thing she could say about the Pullman coach—the food was delicious. The staff also received the magnificent quality of food the paying passengers received, and were well looked after.

If it weren't for the horrid conductor, she would happily transfer to this line. Apart from Henry, everyone, especially Matthew Horton, was nice to her. They were friendly and mostly worked as a team.

Of course, it wasn't an option, since Martha would return soon.

Esther closed her eyes and savored the refreshments Matthew had brought to her. If she hadn't been here, babysitting poor Mrs. Eastlake, she would be clearing dishes or spending time with the passengers of her allotted carriage—the Pullman coach. There was no service in the public carriages, and for that, Esther was grateful. The men, in particular, could be quite rowdy and uncivil. Fights often broke out, and occasionally, a shooting occurred. How people could live that way, she did not know.

She finished up her tea and cake and put the tray aside. A light tap at the door startled her momentarily, then the doctor ducked his head around it. "Everything alright in here?" he asked.

Esther stood and went outside the room to talk to him. "There's been no movement. Mrs. Eastlake is sleeping peacefully." She smiled tentatively then. It was uncanny that a dose of laudanum could have a person sleeping soundly for such a long period.

Doctor Dunne put a hand on Esther's shoulder. "Have no fear. Mrs. Eastlake will awaken." He checked his pocket watch. "Probably not for another thirty minutes. Perhaps longer. Some patients have a lower tolerance and sleep far longer than expected."

Esther nodded. "I suppose it's a good thing? She's not moving about while she's sleeping."

"Precisely," the doctor said. "I'll leave you alone. Please fetch me if there are any issues." He was quickly gone.

Esther was about to return to Mrs. Eastlake's room when she spotted Henry. He was heading her way. She sighed. His face was thunderous, which typical of the conductor.

"Henry," she said as pleasantly as she could muster. "What can I do for you?"

"Get back to your post," he snarled, and Esther took a step back. "I did not give you permission to lounge about with the passengers." He reached out and grabbed her by the arm, yanking Esther toward himself.

"Let go. You're hurting me," Esther said. She was certain there would be a massive bruise on her arm by the end of the day.

Henry's grip didn't budge.

Out of the corner of her eye, Esther saw Matthew storming toward them. She breathed a sigh of relief. "Get your hands off the lady," Matthew said under his breath as he stood over the conductor. "I won't tell you again."

Henry glanced up at him, but didn't loosen his grip. Instead, he tightened it. The pain caused tears to come to her eyes. Matthew took one look at her, then grabbed Henry by the arm, his powerful grip likely to cause even more pain than Henry was imposing on Esther.

"Cut it out," Henry whined, but still didn't let go.

"Last chance, Boswick. Let the lady go right now, or there will be consequences." Matthew meant business. Esther could see it, so why couldn't Henry? Suddenly, Matthew pried Henry's fingers from around her arm, and Esther almost collapsed in relief. "I'm filing charges against you, Boswick.

Now get out of here before I lock you up with Hayes."

Henry rubbed at his arm. "I should be charging you with assault," he said.

"I'm warning you," Matthew told the man. His voice was menacing, and his face enraged. Esther was certain he was being quite restrained, given where they stood.

Suddenly, Henry turned and ran.

"Are you alright?" Matthew asked, concern replacing his previously angry expression. "Would you mind?" he added, not waiting for an answer, but indicating for Esther to show him her bare arm. If it was anyone else asking, she would refuse. But Matthew had nothing but good intentions toward her.

She undid the buttons on her cuff and slid her sleeve up her arm. The fabric rubbing against her skin irritated it. She was loath to even look at the damage that the foul man had done.

Matthew cursed under his breath. "Stay right here," he said, then hurried away.

Esther was bewildered. Where could Matthew have gone in such a hurry? She glanced down at her arm, something she hadn't done until now. She gasped at the damage to her once pristine skin. Large purple bruises already formed, as well as welts, presumably where Henry's nails had dug into her skin. No wonder she was in so much pain.

How could any man inflict such pain on another person, let alone one of his workers? She was beginning to understand why the railway detective hated Henry Boswick so much. It had become obvious to her that Boswick believed himself to be above rules, and also above the law.

It wasn't long before Matthew returned with Doctor Dunne. "Oh, my!" the doctor exclaimed, and Esther glanced down at her arm again. The swelling had become worse, and she couldn't believe how bad it was. "The conductor did this? He needs to be charged!" he said, his voice full of hatred.

"I am laying charges against him," Matthew said firmly. "This behavior is abhorrent. I don't care who his uncle is."

Doctor Dunne led Esther to a chair close to Mrs. Eastlake's room. The woman was still sleeping soundly, according to Matthew, who checked on her for Esther's peace of mind. "We need ice for this," the doctor told Matthew, who hurried to get some.

"I'm certain this is very painful," Doctor Dunne told Esther. "I'm afraid it's going to be bruised and tender for several days. Likely longer." He shook his head then, and Esther was sure he was trying to understand Henry Boswick's actions. Esther was still trying to comprehend it herself. There was no need for the violence. She was beginning to see him through Matthew's eyes. He'd obviously worked with the man for quite some time.

"We'll get the swelling down, then I'll bandage your wound. It won't stop the bruising, but it will stop it throbbing so much." It was clear Doctor Francis Dunne was a good doctor. She'd not told him about the throbbing in her arm, but he instinctively knew.

When Matthew returned with a large bag of ice, it was easy to see he was seething. It was written all over his face. She'd already suspected he was not the man Henry had depicted, and now she knew it for herself. Henry was jealous of this kind-hearted man.

He sat down next to her, holding the ice against her arm, as Doctor Dunne had instructed. It was cold, but numbed the pain, and for that, Esther was grateful. His hands were shaking—even when they were threatened by train robbers, Matthew was not afraid, and was certainly not shaking at all, let alone the way he was now.

She reached over with her good arm and put a hand to his free arm. He glanced down where her hand sat. "Don't be upset," she whispered, and he glanced into her face. "I'll survive." She forced herself to smile then, for Matthew's sake. He was outraged on her behalf, and while she appreciated it, she hated to see him so upset.

"I'm still charging him with assault. If he does it once and gets away with it, he'll do it again."

Esther knew he was right. That was the sort of person the conductor was. He believed himself to be immune from the consequences of his actions. She'd only been on this line a short time, but already, she'd seen it repeatedly.

She'd met his uncle, Alfred Boswick, perhaps twice, and he seemed to be a decent man. What would he think about his railway detective laying assault charges against his nephew? Apart from putting him in a difficult situation, Esther wondered how he would react. She doubted Henry would lose his job.

"The ice has helped tremendously with reducing the swelling," Doctor Dunne said. "I'll now bandage your arm," he said as he began doing so. "This arm must be rested. No waitressing, and definitely no lifting. I'm putting you on light duties for the rest of this trip."

"You can continue to watch over Mrs. Eastlake," Matthew said. "If the weasel bothers you again, I'll put him in the lockup with Hayes."

Esther believed him. Matthew seemed overly upset about Henry manhandling her, and she couldn't fathom it. He was a good man, a decent man, but she felt there was more to it than that. Had Henry Boswick done something like this before? Did that mean he'd got away with it because he was related to the station manager? She certainly hoped not.

"There you are, young lady. All done. If the pain becomes too much, send Matthew to fetch me, and I'll review your injuries." He turned to Matthew then, and they seemed to share a look. Perhaps it was the doctor's way of telling the detective he was counting on him. "I'll check on Mrs. Eastlake now. Are you going to continue sitting with her?" he asked her.

She glanced across at Matthew. "I'd sure like to. What about…" Esther didn't get to finish the sentence since she was interrupted.

"Don't worry about the weasel. He's been warned not to enter this area again. I *will* throw him in the cell with Hayes if he comes near you again, and I told him so."

Esther was convinced he meant every word. It was nice to have a protector, but she wouldn't want to be in Henry's shoes right now.

Chapter Nine

Matthew couldn't believe the gall of Henry Boswick.

How dare he put his hands on a woman? It took all his restraint not to throw the conductor across the room. He only abstained from doing so since Esther would have been harmed in the process. When he saw the damage Henry had caused, Matthew wanted to retaliate on her behalf, but again restrained himself.

He wasn't a violent man, never had been. He did what was needed for his job, which was to protect passengers. But Henry's actions took violence to a whole new level. Esther was a petite person. She was kind, and she was gentle, and was also the most caring person he'd ever come across. With this job, he met new people daily, so that really was saying something.

He glanced down at her hand sitting gently on his arm. Esther was in a power of pain, yet she was more concerned about his wellbeing than her own. Her gentle touch sent heat waves through him, and a shiver down his spine. If he hadn't been sitting down, Matthew was sure it would knock him off his feet.

He wasn't sure why, but simply being near Esther made him feel good. She did things to his soul. Her mere presence made him want to do better. And he wanted to look out for her, not only when Henry was around, but for all time.

The revelation almost made him squirm, but her hand, that continued to sit on his arm, stopped Matthew in his tracks.

When Esther removed her hand and stood, he felt hollow. Bereft even. It was the strangest thing. He'd never felt this way before. But he'd also never been drawn to someone the way he was to her.

She turned to face him and worry etched her face. It made him want to slap the weasel for what he'd done to her.

Matthew forced himself to speak, to reassure her. "You go ahead. I'll keep a close eye on Henry. I've warned him not to venture past my office, and to not come within fifty feet of you." He couldn't help but scowl. "I will protect you, and that's a promise." His heart thudded at her expression. It was one of bewilderment. Had no one ever looked out for her before? Protected her from scum like the vile conductor they were dealing with?

Matthew stood then and glanced about. If Henry came even one step closer than he was supposed to, he was ready. Fury built up inside him all over again.

He watched as Esther stepped into Mrs. Eastlake's room. He was still staring as Doctor Dunne came out of his patient's room.

"Mrs. Eastlake is coming around slowly," he said. "I'll check in on her in about thirty minutes. By then, she might feel like having a light lunch. Soup and sandwiches, perhaps?"

"Leave it with me," Matthew told him. "I'll ensure she doesn't go hungry." It was then it hit him— Esther hadn't eaten lunch either. He'd provided tea and cake, but that wasn't enough to fill her belly. He mentally slapped himself, then hurried to the kitchen to organize her lunch, and prepare them for Mrs. Eastlake for later on.

As he strolled down the corridor toward the kitchen, his heart rate slowed. Until he saw Henry Boswick. Then it thudded. Thankfully, the weasel turned and ran in the other direction.

When Matthew entered the kitchen, he pondered the morning they'd had. It was then he realized he hadn't eaten either. He ordered two meals, and someone else to sit with Mrs. Eastlake while the pair dined in his private office.

Esther watched him cautiously as she ate. Now and again she winced, and he knew she was in pain. It only served to fuel his anger. "The food is good," she said, as though she could read his mind. He noticed long ago she had a knack for distracting people from their concerns. When she was eventually sent back to her own line, Matthew would truly miss her. His heart thudded at the thought.

"It has to be," Matthew said gently. "The money bags who travel in the Pullman coach demand it." He grinned then, and her lips curved into a slight smile.

"Is that what you privately call them?" she asked, clearly trying to hold back a chuckle.

"I do because that's exactly what they are. The majority believe themselves to be better than everyone else, simply because they are loaded."

"And yet, we are the ones who are privileged. We get to spend time in this beautiful carriage, day after day. And…" she paused for a moment or two. "We are paid to do so." She beamed, and Matthew's heart fluttered. He couldn't believe his reactions to this wonderful woman. Esther was a strong woman.

He had no doubt about that. After what Henry did to her, and she still wanted to continue working here.

Still, Henry would not be working here much longer. At least Matthew hoped he wouldn't. The only person who could veto him from laying charges was his uncle, the station manager. Surely he'd had enough of all the complaints that landed on his desk each week?

"Do you know when Martha is returning to work?" she asked quietly. Likely, she wanted to get as far away from Henry as she could. And in as quick a time as possible.

"I don't. I believe she's quite ill, though. She wouldn't stay away this long otherwise." Matthew watched as she took in the information. Esther appeared upset at the news. Was it because of the conductor, who they now knew to be violent? Or was there another reason?

Esther nodded, then went back to her meal. The moment she finished eating, she stood. "I should get back to Mrs. Eastlake," she said firmly. "I don't want Mabel to have issues with Henry like I did."

Matthew could understand why she was concerned, but had already warned Henry to leave the staff alone. His threat of being incarcerated in the tiny cell in his office still stood. Willows Bend wasn't far away now, and they would offload Levi Hayes as quickly as was possible. Even without Hayes there, he would enjoy putting Boswick in that cell. The humiliation alone would be enough to break the weasel. At least he hoped it would.

"What are you grinning about?" Esther asked.

Was he that obvious? "I was dreaming about putting the weasel in the jail cell if he doesn't behave."

She studied him. "You would too. I can just see you manhandling Henry to give him back some of his own misdoings." She chuckled lightly, and a shiver ran through him. What Matthew would give to have her permanently on his line.

Then again, it could surely only lead to disaster. He was already getting far too close to the waitress. In his mind, Esther was destined for far more than spending her days as a waitress. He knew for a fact she would do a much better job than Henry as the conductor for this prestigious carriage. He shook himself mentally.

The railway manager, not to mention the owner, would never allow a woman to become a conductor. But he knew in his heart Esther understood how to run things. Hadn't she taken over Henry's responsibilities when the train robbers had hit? She was also the one who noticed them on their dry run to understand if they were seen.

She could definitely take over from Henry. Whether or not Matthew could convince the station manager was another thing altogether.

The train whistle blew long and loud, alerting him they were about to arrive at Willows Bend. "That's my cue," he said, then reached for the keys to the jail cell. "You go back to Mrs. Eastlake, and out of Henry's view. I'll collect one of the other detectives in case of trouble." He reached for his hat and stormed out of his own office.

It wasn't long before the train pulled into the station, and the two detectives went to the concealed cell. "You'll be out of here shortly," Matthew told Levi Hayes. "I'll make a call to the local constabulary, then you'll be out of my hair."

He closed the secret door again and instructed his colleague to stand guard in his office until Matthew returned.

It didn't take long for the marshals to arrive with a jail cart, and the two detectives marched the cuffed and chained train robber off the train. It meant Matthew could now wipe his hands of the entire episode, and the man in question. Hopefully, the bodies of the gang members they killed, and those shot, would soon be collected.

One piece of dirt gone, now to rid himself of the other.

Chapter Ten

Esther shivered as she watched Levi Hayes being delivered to the police who were waiting on the platform. Today had certainly been eventful. Getting that awful man off the train seemed to lift a weight off her shoulders. It was strange, because she knew he couldn't get to any of the passengers or the staff.

Matthew had seen to that.

Mrs. Eastlake stirred, and Esther spoke quietly, reassuring the elderly woman she was safe and in expert hands with Doctor Dunne. "You must be starving," she told the passenger. "We have arranged food for you. The doctor said he would pop in to ensure you are well."

"Thank you, dear," the patient said. "I don't know what I would have done without you. Esther Walters, you are an absolute godsend," she said as she tried to sit up.

Esther stood and helped the woman into a sitting position. She winced as pain ran down her arm.

"What have you done?" Mrs. Eastlake demanded, her lips pulled into a straight line.

Staring at the woman, Esther didn't know what to say. "I…my arm is bruised," she said firmly. "Doctor Dunne bandaged it for me."

Mrs. Eastlake studied her then. "Did that evil Henry Boswick accost you?"

Esther was stunned. "Why would you say that?" She wouldn't lie, but neither did she want to admit the conductor had assaulted her.

"Because I've seen him do it to other people, that's why." She glanced toward the door then. "Oh, Mr. Horton. Thank you again for finding me. I don't know what would have happened otherwise."

His glance went from Mrs. Eastlake to Esther, and back to the older woman again. How much had he heard of the conversation? "To be honest, Esther was the one who realized you were missing. So you need to thank her, not me." He stepped toward the bed then. "I'll arrange some food for you. Doc says something light—soup and sandwiches perhaps? Or scrambled eggs. Your choice."

"Soup and sandwiches would be perfect. Thank you, Mr. Horton."

He nodded, then quickly left, returning a short time later. The tray he carried also had a pot of tea, along with a pretty cup and saucer, and a sweet pastry.

Matthew sat down on the edge of the bed once he was certain Mrs. Eastlake was comfortable and happy. "Now what's this about witnessing Boswick assaulting other people?"

"Other people?" She turned to Esther. "Oh, my dear girl. I am so very sorry. I should have reported it before, but who is going to believe an old lady like me?"

"We believe you," Matthew said firmly. "And I'll make sure he doesn't do it again."

Esther hoped Matthew was right. Henry needed to be stopped. Those in powerful positions could not be allowed to get away with abusive behavior. Knowing Matthew Horton, she was certain he would follow through on his promise to put a stop to the horrible man's abhorrent actions.

As though on cue, her arm throbbed. Without thinking, she lifted her other hand and rubbed it along the bandaged area.

Matthew studied her. "Should I get Doctor Dunne?" he asked, his voice full of concern.

Her heart thudded. Matthew had an important position, and his time was better fulfilled elsewhere. "I'm fine," she lied.

"Oh, Mr. Horton," Mrs. Eastlake said. "You didn't bring tea for Esther." She looked concerned, but didn't need to be.

"Matthew and I have not long dined, and I had a pot of tea then," Esther said. The sly smile that came to the woman's lips told Esther she'd said far too much.

When she glanced across at Matthew, he was grinning. Esther frowned. Those around them saw far too much into the time they spent together. They were work colleagues and nothing more. Her heart fluttered, forcing Esther to wonder why.

As she studied him, Matthew rubbed a hand across his unshaven chin. He was handsome, in a rugged way, but that was not what drew her to him. It was his confidence, not to mention his kind heart. He had a heart of gold, and his morals were above reproach. If Matthew said he would do something, he did it. She fully expected when they arrived back in Timberlake Junction, he would apply to lay charges against Henry Boswick. Whether his uncle would allow him to follow through was another thing altogether.

"That was delicious. Thank you, Mr. Horton," Mrs. Eastlake said. "I'm rather looking forward to my hospital visit. I'll be waited on hand and foot. Much like I am now," she said. "Of course, having the pain alleviated will be wonderful."

Esther pitied the older woman. According to Matthew, she was a widow, and rode the trains regularly to fill in her days. Who would guess she would trip and injure herself to this extent? At least she would be in her hometown of Helena.

"I'm certain you'll be well cared for there," Esther said. "It's the biggest hospital in the area and has an excellent reputation."

Until now, Esther hadn't really thought much about getting old. It must have been awful losing her husband of decades. Had she refrained from marrying for that reason? When Esther's father died, Mother had mourned for many years until her own death. The heartache was tremendous, watching her mother slowly dying of a broken heart. *But what of the years in between?* That voice in her head was right. Her parents had a love deeper than anything she'd ever witnessed before.

Esther wanted that for herself and wasn't prepared to accept anything less. She glanced across at Matthew again. Her heart fluttered yet again, despite her efforts to deny she was attracted to the man.

"I'm going to get the doc," Matthew said, then glanced at her arm. Without even realizing it, Esther was massaging her throbbing arm. The dreadful conductor certainly had a lot to answer for. She only hoped the detective could put a stop to his abhorrent and dangerous behavior for the sake of his other potential victims.

Esther chatted with Mrs. Eastlake while the older woman finished her meal. She was a lovely person, and had lived a full life of travel, balls, and adventure with her rich husband. No wonder she loved traveling on the trains. Although some might see it as boring, there was always someone to talk to and share their life adventures.

It wasn't long before Doctor Dunne arrived. "Miss Walters," he said firmly. "You were supposed to let me know if you were in pain. Come with me."

Esther scowled at Matthew. He grinned. "I'll sit with Mrs. Eastlake," he said, and claimed Esther's seat.

Doing her best not to wince as the bandage was removed, Esther fought back the tears that came into her eyes. It was the most pain she could ever recall experiencing.

"I apologize, but I need to do this." He flinched when the bandage was completely off. Doctor Dunne then reached into his medical bag. "This is witch hazel gel. It will help reduce the bruises and hopefully lessen the pain." He opened the bottle and was about to rub it into Esther's arm. "This is going to hurt a bit."

She braced herself, knowing if the doctor told her it would be painful, it would be. His hands were gentle, and thankfully, the discomfort was minimal. Then he re-bandaged her arm.

"Boswick needs to be punished for this. The man is an animal," he muttered. He then accompanied her back to Mrs. Eastlake's room. "Horton, make a note. I would be pleased to stand up in court about the injuries Miss Walters received at the hand of that poor excuse for a man. This has to stop."

"I'll do that," Matthew told him. "Thank you for all your help during this trip. I don't know what we would have done without you."

Doctor Dunne nodded briefly, then was gone.

Esther wondered if the conductor would ever be charged or even end up in court. Somehow, she thought not.

~*~

It was a bitter-sweet goodbye with Mrs. Eastlake as they waited for her to be taken from the train and transferred to the ambulance.

Matthew accompanied Doctor Dunne to the woman's room, where, following the doctor's orders, gently put his hands underneath her. He supported her broken leg the way he was told, then carried her out to the waiting ambulance.

"Ooooh," she said excitedly. "I haven't been carried like this since my wedding day."

Matthew grinned, and Esther held back a chuckle. The doctor was clearly amused and tried not to grin, but lost the battle.

"I will see you at the hospital," Doctor Dunne told her.

"You will? That would be wonderful," Mrs. Eastlake told him.

"Helena is the hospital I am based at," he said. "I am the head orthopedic surgeon there."

Esther was pleased for Mrs. Eastlake, but not at all surprised. It was clear Doctor Dunne was highly qualified, and knew exactly what he was doing. Without him, the woman's leg may have been deformed for the rest of her life.

She followed them out to the platform. The ambulance was ready to take the patient to the hospital. It was another weight lifted off Esther's shoulders. Now there was only one problem to face on the trip back.

Henry Boswick.

The last thing Esther wanted to do was work under the man, but now she would have to do so.

Chapter

Eleven

Matthew turned to face Esther the moment Mrs. Eastlake was taken away in the ambulance. Her distress was clear almost immediately.

She had endured far more than anyone should have to suffer at work. For him, it was his job, and they paid him handsomely for it. Esther was a completely different story.

He moved to her side and put an arm around her. Esther glanced up at him, but said nothing. He could feel her shaking. "Tell me what's wrong," he said, then pulled her into his arms.

Esther glanced about. They were in public and he was holding her in a way he had no right to do. Instead of pushing him away as he thought she might, she rested her head against his chest.

"I'm afraid to go back and work with Henry," she said so quietly he could barely hear her.

Matthew held her at arm's length. "You won't be doing that, I can assure you." He hadn't told her what he'd planned and then carried out, but perhaps he should have. "I have laid charges against Henry. The marshals are on the train interviewing him now, and they will want to interview you as well." He brushed Esther's hair back off her face. "They will take Mrs. Eastlake's statement when she is well enough to provide one. We can only hope the weasel will be in jail during our trip back to Timberlake Junction."

He felt Esther's relief as she sighed against him. Matthew rubbed his hands across her back, the movement soothing to him. He only hoped it did the same for her. "Thank you," she whispered. "The man is a danger to anyone he comes in contact with."

Matthew knew it was complicated. They had a two-day stopover in Helena while the train was cleaned and readied for the return trip. Their rooms were booked, and their luggage would have already been delivered on their behalf. "We will stay at the Travelers End Hotel. It's comfortable and clean. We always stay there."

"I feel better knowing you'll be there, too. What about Henry?" Esther's face was a testament to her anguish, and Matthew felt bad for her.

"There is every possibility the weasel will have accommodations of a different kind." He took great pleasure in knowing that dreadful man would be locked away in a cold jail cell in Helena. That way, he could cause no more harm.

Esther glanced up at him, her relief clear. "I never thought I'd think this way, but I'm truly glad. After what he did to me, I am afraid for my safety."

Matthew continued to embrace Esther for a few more minutes, and enjoyed every moment. Despite knowing he shouldn't.

"Do you know who I am?" the familiar voice shouted at the two marshals who accompanied him. "My uncle will have your jobs for this." Henry continued to cause a scene as they dragged him in handcuffs from the train. Matthew refrained from showing his pleasure at what was going on. It was well past time Henry Boswick was made accountable for his actions.

"What will his uncle say about Henry's arrest?" Esther asked quietly.

Matthew's arms tightened around her. "I spoke with him briefly from the manager's office at the station. He agreed Henry should be charged, and an investigation instigated." He glanced down at the woman making herself more than a little comfortable in his arms. "I was tasked with replacing Henry for the return trip."

The look on Esther's face told him she was concerned. Was there another worker on the train who had caused her misery? "He also mentioned Martha won't be returning. Unfortunately, she died yesterday." Matthew was shocked by the news the station manager had shared. The woman was not what he'd call old. She couldn't have been more than forty-five. "I'll come with you to collect anything still on the train, then we'll head to the hotel."

He glanced down at Esther. Sadness shrouded her face despite not knowing Martha except by name. "I'm sorry about Martha," she said, and he appreciated it.

They boarded the train again, where Esther retrieved her reticule, and Matthew ensured his firearms were securely locked in his office. Not that he had any doubt—he was the only one with a key, and he was always extremely vigilant when it came to weapons.

He heard Esther's sigh of relief once they were outside again. He led her to their hotel, which was within walking distance.

~*~

"This is lovely," Esther said as she sat back against the comfortable sofa in the public area. Matthew reveled in the fact there were few individual chairs available, and they sat close together. He'd arranged for coffee for himself, and a pot of tea for Esther—her preference. It wouldn't be long before supper was served, but he still insisted they indulge in sweet pastries.

The Travelers End Hotel was not the most upmarket hotel in Helena, but it was definitely one of Matthew's favorites. Not that he'd stayed elsewhere, because this is where the staff always stayed for the two-day stopover. "We're always well looked after here," he said. "And why wouldn't they? The railway pays handsomely for all the staff to stay each week. It's a goldmine to them."

He smiled for the first time since they'd arrived. Now settled, he knew there were no more problems for him to solve. The weasel was locked away, and Esther was safe. Not to mention the other female workers. They were Boswick's target. He'd found no reports of men being attacked. The weasel would only target the vulnerable, and he knew men would fight back. They'd likely flatten the obnoxious man. What a pity he didn't try it with Matthew—he knew what the outcome would have been.

Esther sipped her tea as she glanced around. "The décor here is truly beautiful." Matthew supposed it was. He hadn't been to many hotels over the years.

His only visits were related to work. "It's far better than what we have on my regular line."

Matthew studied her for mere seconds. "Would you be open to changing that?" he asked tentatively. "Coming over to the Helena line, I mean." He sipped his coffee, then watched her over the top of his mug.

He could see the confusion on her face. "Permanently, do you mean? Or until they find a replacement for Martha?" Her last words were full of emotion, which only went to prove to Matthew how truly caring Esther was.

"Both." The moment he'd said it, Matthew knew that was confusing. "Let me start again." He took a fortifying breath. "I've been tasked with securing a temporary replacement for Henry until it's known whether he will face assault charges. I want you to take over." Esther stared at him, her face full of amazement.

"Women..." She seemed to choose her words carefully. "We can't be conductors," she finally said.

"Why is that?" Oh, he knew what she was about to say, but wanted to hear it from Esther.

"I...um." She smacked her mouth closed before opening it again. "We just can't."

"There's no one else on the train I trust to run the Pullman coach. Tell me you'll do it?" He almost pleaded with her, and Esther studied him for long minutes before answering again.

"Are you certain about this? It seems rather extreme."

He didn't like to see her frown. She'd done far too much of that lately. "I am certain. And yes, it's extreme, but right now, there is no choice. Say yes, and I can get the ball rolling."

Esther stared at him again and blinked. Several times. Her hands shook as she tried to lift her tea. Matthew covered them and immediately felt the effect of doing so.

Their eyes met, and he was certain she'd felt it too. "Yes," she whispered, but didn't force his hands away.

Matthew knew exactly what was going on, but it was the last thing he wanted. His job and women didn't go well together.

Twelve

Esther shivered as Matthew's hands covered hers.

Her feelings for him had been building from the moment they first met, despite the word of warning from Henry. The cautions she now knew to be untrue. That she had kept her distance, and felt contempt toward him in the beginning, played on her mind. "I'm truly sorry," she whispered, then forced her hands out of his grip.

Matthew stared at her. "Sorry for what?" He frowned, no doubt trying to work out her cryptic words. "You did nothing wrong."

She wished that were true. "I believed Henry when he told me not to trust you. That you are a…" Esther stumbled with her words. Did she really want to say them out loud? She swallowed back her emotions at the thought of how she'd initially responded to him.

"Womanizer. I know the lies the weasel spread about me. They were difficult to ignore." He reached out and covered her hand. "That's not me. My job is not conducive to a relationship."

Esther knew he was right, but it didn't stop her feelings for him. "How long have you been a railway detective?" It was surely a long time— Matthew knew exactly what needed to be done in any situation.

"Here in Montana, since the railway began. I worked in Ohio for several years before that. It would have to be close to ten years in total. Before that, I was a sheriff in a small town for a few years. That life was too boring for me, but what I wouldn't do to have it back now."

She saw the regret on his face. But would they have met if Matthew still worked as a small-town sheriff? Esther was convinced they wouldn't have. "Too many robberies? Or because of Henry and his awful behavior?"

He shrugged. "Mostly Henry, I guess. He's only been working on this line for a relatively short time. A matter of months? Maybe six, or it could be more. He definitely does not know what he's doing."

Esther licked her lips. She wanted to agree, but felt it wasn't her place.

"Something you want to add?" Matthew demanded.

She shook her head, but he pierced her with his gaze. "Only I reiterate what you said. He's disorganized and doesn't understand the way things work on the railway."

"But you do." It was a statement, and Esther knew that's what Matthew meant it to be. "It's exactly the reason I want you to be acting conductor on the trip back."

Esther still wasn't certain it was the right thing to do. Many other staff members had worked that line far longer than she had. They probably knew as much as Esther did. Would they be put out? And what would the station manager say when he found out she took over his nephew's position, even if it was temporary?

It was all too much. So many awful things had happened over a short period of time. It made her shiver.

"Esther," Matthew said quietly. "It's temporary. Alfred Boswick, the station manager, has approved your appointment."

"You named me to him? He knows a woman will do the job?" She found it difficult to believe the station manager of all people would approve of having a woman take over the job of conductor. Even if it was only short term.

"He knows the railway is in a difficult situation. If Henry is charged, which is highly likely, the railway could be sued. There could be a mass walkout of staff as well, and that would cause chaos." Matthew studied her before he spoke again. "We are both relying on you to ensure the passengers on the return journey have a safe and satisfactory trip. I know you can do it."

Could she do it? Esther thought back to how many of Henry's responsibilities she'd overseen during the robbery. How the man had cowered in the butler's pantry while she took over notifying the other detectives on the train. Not to mention she'd had to organize the waitresses at meal times. The man was a fool of massive proportions. If it wasn't for family connections, he would never have been given the job.

"You told him Henry attacked me." It was a statement, not a question, and they both knew it. Esther straightened her back and firmed up her resolve. "You're right, I can do it. I know I can. There is a problem, though. I don't have the right attire for the position."

"Already sorted. Tomorrow we go into town and acquire whatever you need. Don't worry, the railway is paying for it."

Esther nodded her agreement, but was still apprehensive. Would the other staff accept her authority with Henry gone? She already had their respect, but now she needed their loyalty.

"That's settled," Matthew said as he stood. "There's enough time for a short stroll before supper. That is, if you're interested."

He smiled at her, and Esther's heart fluttered. It was probably the worst idea he could have had. At least on the train, they each had their jobs to do, and were often apart. Off the train, here in Helena, they were thrown together.

The biggest worry was knowing where it might lead. Even worse was realizing she was looking forward to spending time with the enticing railway detective.

~*~

"I've walked past this store many times," Matthew said, as they strolled down the main street of Helena the next morning. "I've never been inside, but this is where we'll get your uniform."

"Is it really necessary? I mean, it's only going to be needed for this one journey." More's the pity since she had enjoyed the change of scenery.

"It truly is. The passengers need to know who is in charge." He reached up and patted her hand. Esther had enjoyed walking side by side with Matthew

Horton, even if she had to tilt her head to look into his face. He was a proper gentleman, despite having to deal with criminals and ruffians occasionally. "The passengers love you. Take Mrs. Kilberry, for example. I'm willing to bet she's already been in the owner's ear."

"Do you really think so?" Esther thought the elderly woman could be all talk, but no action.

Matthew chuckled. "She's a woman of her word. I have no doubt she's already let her opinion be known." His expression became serious then. "You may not realize, but she is the widow of Kilberry Textiles owner. It's a huge national corporation." He rubbed his thumb across his fingers, indicating they were made of money. Suddenly, he leaned in. "Money bags," he said, then laughed.

Esther could listen to that sound all day. It put joy in her heart, and a skip in her step. Despite all the upset and terrifying experiences recently, she had enjoyed her time on the journey to Helena. She knew it was all down to Matthew Horton. He was a man of honor and integrity. She felt safe around him and knew he could be trusted.

"Let's do this," she said, as they stepped into the enormous store. It wasn't long before Esther was outfitted and looked as though she'd been doing the job forever.

#

#

Matthew stared at Esther as she strolled past him in her conductor's uniform. Not that they catered for women in the role, but they'd improvised.

Black dress pants became a black skirt. The white shirt and black jacket with a black bowtie were the same as the men would wear. To finish it off, the official railway conductor's hat.

He continued to stare until his breath left his body. If he thought she looked good in her waitress uniform, it was nothing compared to this one. The fact was, Esther Walters stacked up no matter how she dressed.

She was beautiful inside and out, and he'd known it from the moment they met. It was an unfortunate fact that Henry had spouted his lies and tainted

Esther's view of him. Matthew hoped by now she realized they were lies, and he was not that person the weasel had portrayed.

"What do you think?" Esther said, standing in front of him.

His eyes wandered from the top of her head to her toes. He loved what he saw. "What I think," he said as he came to stand in front of her, "is you look beautiful. Perhaps too beautiful to wear that outfit in front of the passengers."

She beamed. "Are you jealous?" she asked jokingly.

Was he? Matthew licked his lips. He already knew he was becoming far too fond of his new work companion, but could he stand there and deny it? Instead, he reached for her hands. "To be truthful," he said quietly so no one else in the store could hear, "I think I am."

Her eyes opened wide in astonishment, and without another word she hurried back to the changing room. Matthew sat down where he'd previously waited, pondering his words. It was a bad idea to let her know how he felt, especially since they would work closely together on the trip back home. It was a relatively short trip, but he already knew what could happen in such a period of time. Their lives were already entwined because of the circumstances they found themselves in.

Esther hurried out of the changing room and went to the front counter with her newly acquired outfit. Matthew joined her there. "We need two of each," he told the cashier. He felt Esther staring at him, but said nothing more. "Please deliver everything to Miss Esther Walters at the Travelers End Hotel by nine tomorrow morning at the latest. And bill it to Timberlake Railways."

"Yes, Sir," the cashier said.

As they walked away, he noticed the curiosity on Esther's face. "Why two of each? I'll only be doing the one trip in this capacity."

"Orders from the boss. Just in case, he said." Matthew shrugged then. "Who knows how long it will be before they release the weasel from custody?" The longer the better, he felt like saying, but kept his thoughts to himself. Matthew knew from the moment he met the man, Henry was trouble. His uncle might have thought it would be good for his nephew, but it wasn't good for those he worked with. Especially the women he'd assaulted. The repercussions could continue for a very long time.

Esther glanced about as they made their way out of the large department store. "Do you want to explore, or return to the hotel?" he asked, preferring to show her around, but not voicing his opinion.

She turned and smiled at him. Matthew's heart fluttered. "I'd love to explore," she said. "Even better when it's with someone you l…" Her words trailed and he wondered what she was going to say. "Like," she said hesitantly.

Was she going to say *love*? Surely not? Matthew knew he had feelings for the woman standing beside him, but he was confused about what those feelings were. Was it love he felt, or was it merely friendship? For him, it seemed to be more than friendship, but for Esther, was it more? He may never know. "I like you, too," he said, then wished he'd said a whole lot more. After all, if he wanted their friendship to bloom into something completely different, he had to let his thoughts be known.

"Esther," he said warily, then thought the better of it. When he glanced at her, Esther's face was turned toward the sun. He watched as she basked in the warmth of it and smiled. She was unique, her own person, and he loved that about her. "Why don't we head for the park? There's a pergola there where we can sit, or we can stroll through the gardens and take in the nature."

A smile came to her face. "That sounds wonderful. I enjoy nature and the fresh air. And Matthew," she said, reaching for his hand. "I enjoy being with you."

Her last words floored him. "You do? I enjoy spending time with you as well," he said. "Especially away from work."

Esther was now beaming, and his heart filled with joy. Matthew wasn't sure what was going on between them, but he knew it was something special. "It's this way," he said, pointing in the direction they needed to go. She still held onto his hand, and he wasn't going to protest the fact.

~*~

The moment they sat down in the pergola, Matthew knew it was a bad idea. They were near to each other, not that they hadn't done that before. Here they were totally alone. The area was fairly isolated away from the main part of town, and it was quiet. Peaceful.

"I love it here," Esther said. "Thank you for bringing me here."

She was right—it was peaceful. The only sounds that could be heard were the birds twittering in the trees, and the water in the fast-flowing stream that wound through the park. The pergola was mostly in shadow, but Esther had chosen a spot where the sunlight streamed through. It wasn't large, but it was big enough to accommodate them both. He had to admit, the warmth of the sun was pleasing. Especially considering they spent most of their days on a train with no fresh air and no sunlight.

"I've never been here before today," he admitted. "It's not much fun exploring alone." He rarely left the hotel on their days off, instead either staying in his room or socializing with the other workers. The latter was rare.

Her eyebrows rose in question. "I'm not one for socializing much," he told her. "I live for my work."

Esther glanced down at their entwined hands sitting in her lap. "I'm the same—work, have a couple of days off, work again, days off again. It's never ending."

"Only now you've been thrown in the deep end through no fault of your own." It was true, and he knew it. He wouldn't tell Esther, but he was certain Mrs. Kilberry had already spoken to the owner of Timberlake Railways. It had to be the reason Alfred Boswick put her in the position of conductor. How long it would last was another thing.

"I won't pretend I'm not terrified," she said quietly.

Matthew stared at her until she turned away. "You know what you're doing. I know what the weasel did during the attempted robbery—things always get back to me," he said. "While he cowered in the butler's pantry, you took over. Not that I'm surprised."

Her eyes flickered up to look at him, and heat came into her cheeks. "I only did what needed to be done," she whispered.

"It's the very reason you've been offered this temporary position," Matthew told her. She closed her eyes then and basked in the sun again. The more he knew Esther Walters, the more enamored he became with her. If he wasn't careful, he'd fall in love with her.

Even now he'd had to resist the urge to kiss her, but they were totally alone, and the last thing he wanted to do was compromise her.

To heck with it all—he couldn't resist. He leaned across and pulled Esther to him. He stared into her hazel-colored eyes and glanced at her lips. She didn't protest and didn't push him away. Instead, her arms went up around his neck.

Before he knew it, Matthew was kissing her, and Esther giving as good as she got.

Chapter

Fourteen

Esther melted in Matthew's arms. She had longed for this moment, but also hoped it never happened. She knew once it did happen, there would be no going back. For her, anyway.

She heard herself sigh, and then she moaned. Matthew chuckled. She pushed him away. "That's just rude," she said, keeping her hands against his chest in a half-hearted effort to distance herself.

Matthew grinned as he glanced down at her. Suddenly, his smile dropped. "I'm sorry," he said firmly. "I should not have done that." He slid away from her on the wooden bench.

"I'm glad you did," Esther said as she frowned. "But I guess you didn't enjoy it the way I did." She stood then and walked away. Hopefully, she would find her way back to the hotel herself.

"Esther," Matthew called to her, but with his one step to every two of hers, he was quickly behind her. He snaked an arm around her waist and pulled her up against him. "I did enjoy kissing you. I truly did." His fingers pushed her collar aside, and he kissed her shoulder. A shiver went through her.

She relaxed against him, much to her disappointment. They were work colleagues, after all. "What will people say?" she whispered, knowing it wouldn't look good. His lips lifted from her skin, and disappointment filled her.

"You should know by now I don't care what people think." He went back to kissing her shoulder, and a shudder went through her. Esther heard Matthew chuckle. "What would you like to do now?" he asked, and her mind went to places it shouldn't.

"Stay here?" She was very unsure of the new level their relationship had taken. Not that she'd been forced, because she hadn't. Her uncertainty came because of their close working relationship. Although now that Henry was gone, she wouldn't be working so closely with Matthew.

He spun Esther around in his arms and stared into her face for so long, she almost squirmed. "There's not a lot to do in Helena," he said as he stared at her lips. "Unless you're into the theater scene."

She shook her head. That wasn't her scene at all. "I'm more of a homebody. I like the quiet life, and spending time with the people I love."

Matthew frowned then. "Is there someone at home you love?" he asked, his face shrouded in curiosity. Did he think she had a boyfriend or husband hidden away somewhere? That she would kiss him if that were the case?

Indignity filled her. Esther pulled out of his arms and stormed away. As she glanced about, she did not know how to get back to the hotel, but someone could surely tell her.

"Esther." Her name on his lips hung in the air as her heart pounded. She came to a crossroads in the park and didn't know which way to go. The area was thick with trees and foliage, and she could easily get lost. Her heart rate kicked up. She heard footsteps behind her, but ignored them and hurried toward her goal.

The hotel.

Without warning, hands reached out and grabbed at her, and she fell to the ground. Her reticule gripped tightly in her hands, she realized it wasn't Matthew who had reached for her, but some dirty street urchin who wanted her money.

Why had she run? She was in a far worse situation now than she ever dreamed possible. Even on the train, during the robbery, she wasn't in this much danger. There were men all around her with firearms. Men who knew what they were doing.

This scenario was completely different. This time, her very existence was in jeopardy.

Grubby hands reached for her reticule. Esther gripped it even tighter. She heard running—it was like music to her ears. "Get your grubby hands off the lady and get out of here. Otherwise, I will personally drag you all the way to the sheriff's office."

The attacker was gone in a heartbeat.

Esther's relief at Matthew's presence was palpable. She still lay on the ground and still clutched her reticule. He was by her side in seconds and stared down at her. His annoyance was obvious. "Why did you run off?" he asked abruptly. Without waiting for an answer, he reached out to help her to her feet. "Are you hurt?" he asked when she didn't move.

She shook her head. "Only my pride." Had she been alone, she may have cried. For no other reason but frustration with herself. Esther brushed herself off as she stood. So far, so good. Everything seemed to be fine.

"Do *not* do that again," Matthew demanded. "The park itself is safe. You ventured into the forest— that's a whole different scenario. It's a hub for vagrants and criminals." He put an arm around her waist, and glancing about led her away from the dangerous area she'd ventured into.

When they were back in familiar territory, Esther began to relax. Her entire body ached from the stress and the fall. Soon they were on the main street of Helena again, and he led her to a wooden bench where they sat.

"I'm sorry," he said. "I'm not sure what I said to make you run, but I meant nothing by it."

She stared at him. "Your words insinuated I had a boyfriend at home. Or a husband." Esther glanced up at him. Matthew was frowning. "I would never do that," she whispered.

"You wouldn't, I know you wouldn't," he said gently. "I meant no such thing. I wondered about your family, your parents."

Esther could see she'd upset him, not only by her actions, but also by her words. "I'm sorry for running. I should never have jumped to conclusions."

Matthew scooted a little closer, then put an arm around her waist. "We can sit here for a while, if that's what you want." He glanced at the variety of shops nearby, then suddenly he smiled. "I see a café. Cake would be nice."

Esther chuckled. "It certainly would." And it was bound to lift both their spirits. Matthew stood, then reached for her hands. He helped Esther to her feet. Once standing, they were so close she could feel his breath on her cheek. His eyes roamed to her lips, but she turned her face away.

Kissing Matthew in the park where they were alone was one thing. Doing it out here in the open was quite another.

"Shall we go?" he asked, but didn't wait for an answer. He led Esther to the cake shop across the road and ordered the most luxurious looking cakes for each of them. Esther savored every bite.

~*~

"I've had a great day," Matthew said when they arrived back at the Travelers End Hotel. They'd wandered around town after their refreshments, and finally headed for home. It was almost time for supper, but they would have time to freshen up.

As they passed the front desk, the clerk caught Esther's attention. "Miss Walters," he said. "A package arrived for you. I had it delivered to your room."

"Thank you. I appreciate it," she said, then opened her reticule.

Matthew covered her hand with his. "I've got this," he said, then handed the man a bank note. As they walked away, he explained the tip would be covered in the expenses he claimed.

They walked up the carpeted stairs together, and when they reached Esther's room, Matthew turned to face her. "I've never enjoyed the stopovers so much," he said, pulling her close against him. "It's all thanks to you."

Glancing up at him, Esther could tell he was more relaxed. There were fewer frown lines, and his face was different. The worry he'd endured lately had left him, and it was easy to see. "I'm glad," she said, and he leaned down and kissed her. Esther leaned into him, dropping her reticule to her feet on the floor. Her arms went around his neck, and his warmth flooded her. How anyone could believe this man was a womanizer, she would never know.

Why Henry would spread such lies, she would never understand. Except the man was spiteful. Matthew didn't suffer fools easily, and perhaps that was Henry's motivation. Either way, it certainly didn't help the conductor earn the respect of his workers. Or should that be the former conductor? Things did not look good for Henry Boswick, and it was all of his own doing.

Esther heard someone shuffling past them in the narrow hallway and stepped back. "I should go," she said. "I need to freshen up."

Matthew grinned. "I'll collect you, in, say, fifteen minutes?"

"I would like that," Esther said, then pulled the key from her reticule. She unlocked the door and hurried inside. What she wouldn't give to have another uninterrupted day with the railway detective. Tomorrow, they would begin their return trip with Esther as the conductor of the Pullman coach. That needed to be her focus until they returned to Timberlake Junction. Distractions would be her downfall.

That included matters of the heart.

Chapter Fifteen

Last night's supper had gone well, and he had kissed Esther goodnight at her door. She hadn't resisted, and she melted into him. Still, Matthew sensed something had changed.

It was almost time to leave the hotel and return to the daily grind on the railway. He felt privileged to serve on the Pullman coach—some of the public passengers were difficult to manage, as he'd found when they were in the midst of their *drill*. Matthew did not know how the detectives in those carriages managed on a day-to-day basis.

He finished packing his overnight bag and headed toward the door. Someone would be along shortly to collect all their bags and deliver them to the train. By the time the staff arrived, their belongings would be safely stored.

There was a light tap on the door. The porter was earlier than expected. He opened the door, ready to hand the bag over. Except it wasn't the porter— Esther stood in front of him.

She looked resplendent in her conductor's uniform. Almost regal. The outfit suited her perfectly, but a bit of color would make it even better. "Good morning," he said, waiting for her smile.

It didn't come.

"Good morning," she said pensively. Esther was clearly nervous.

Reaching for her hand, Matthew dropped the bag at his feet. "You'll be fine," he said. "You know the job, and the staff already know you. What could go wrong?"

She licked her lips, and his lips twitched. He wanted nothing less than to pull her close and kiss her senseless. It was a sad state of affairs that people were milling around them. There were porters, and there were hotel guests. Not to mention the cleaners already working on the rooms that had recently been vacated.

Esther glanced around her. A few of the waitresses and other railway staff acknowledged them on their way to the dining room. Breakfast was now being served. Despite the enormous meal they consumed last night, his belly was protesting. "Are you ready to eat?" Matthew asked, trying to distract himself from her enticing lips. "It won't be long after breakfast we have to leave."

Esther stared at him with sad eyes. "Of course," she said, then turned away, ready to conquer the stairs. His heart thudded. She was distancing herself from him. Matthew could feel it in his very being.

"Esther, wait up," he called as he shoved his bag back inside his room and locked the door. He quickly caught up, but she didn't acknowledge his presence. When they arrived in the dining room, they were taken to their allocated table where they were seated with the other railway workers.

It meant private conversations were out of the question. It did, however, give him an opportunity to announce Esther's temporary position. "Everyone, listen up," Matthew said loud enough only those at their table could hear. "There's been a slight change of plan. Henry Boswick is indisposed, and the station manager has asked Esther to take his place."

"I saw the marshals dragging him away," one chef said with a sneer. "Best thing ever."

Several other workers agreed, and many, especially the women, appeared relieved. Matthew shushed everyone, then explained they had not charged Henry with anything. At this point, it was an investigation.

Soon their food arrived, and everyone concentrated on eating.

Matthew did note, however, not one person complained or whined about Esther taking over. He reached for her hand under the table. She was shaking, and he squeezed her hand tight for mere seconds, then she pulled it away. Esther glanced at him, her eyes sad, then ate her food.

One by one, the other workers went back to their rooms. They would soon be back on board the train, where they would be expected to work almost non-stop. It was a hard slog, but someone had to do it. At least they were paid well for their endeavors.

"Esther," Matthew said when she stood and looked as though she would leave without him. "Is something wrong?" He reached for her hand, but she pulled it away. His heart thudded. Had she changed her mind about the two of them?

"This was a mistake," she said quietly, and dropped back into the chair next to him. "We are coworkers. I should never have led you on." Her eyes shone with unshed tears, and Matthew knew this was not what she wanted.

"Has anyone said something to you? About us?" He felt fury burn its way up inside of him. No one had the right to dictate what they could do or who they should see.

Esther shook her head. "Nothing like that. I have, however, seen the looks. A few of the workers have guessed, I'm certain. Besides, knowing Henry, after seeing us together, he would have spread rumors."

Of course he would. The weasel was renowned for rumor mongering. Matthew was certain he did it to take the focus off his own failings. As disappointed as he felt right now, Esther was right. "Neither of us will have time to spend together until we arrive back at Timberlake Junction, anyway. We can talk again, then."

Esther nodded, but seemed far more distant than he would have liked. Still, she had a lot on her mind. Her new job and responsibilities, ensuring the workers followed orders, and making sure a whole new set of passengers were well cared for.

Matthew stood. "I'll walk you to your room," he said. This time he didn't reach for her hand, and his heart felt hollow.

Was it the end before they'd even begun? Matthew certainly hoped not. He'd opened his heart to Esther, and knew it would shatter into an unbreakable mess if he lost her.

~*~

To Matthew's surprise, Mrs. Kilberry was waiting to board the train when they arrived. A few passengers lingered on the platform, waiting for the staff to arrive. As part of Esther's new position, she welcomed all the passengers, and checked the tickets of those boarding the Pullman coach. A smile crossed her lips the moment she saw Mrs. Kilberry. "Good morning," Esther said, and reached for the older woman's ticket. Not that she needed to. The woman was a regular. But Esther needed to be seen to be doing her job.

Mrs. Kilberry beamed. "I am so pleased to see my advice has been heeded," she said, then accepted Esther's help climbing the steps. Matthew was convinced their wealthy passenger would do exactly what she said, and talk to Wallace Steel, the railways owner. "I told him about you, and Wallace agreed you needed to be doing what you do best." Even when she was at the top of the steps, Mrs. Kilberry didn't stop. "I surely didn't expect him to go to these lengths." She leaned in and attempted to whisper, but Matthew heard every word. "You deserve it, my dear, and that uniform looks wonderful on you. Don't you agree, Mr. Horton?" she asked. Without waiting for an answer, their energetic passenger headed toward her room. The same one she demanded every time she traveled.

Esther glanced across at him and smiled. If Mrs. Kilberry believed she'd influenced the change in position, they would let her.

The other passengers alighted the train without incident, and they were soon on their way. Matthew headed to his office and sat behind his desk. It was going to be a long trip back to Timberlake Junction.

He already missed Esther, and there was nothing he could do about it. They hadn't even left the station yet, and he was pining for her.

As he stood glancing out the window of his office, there was a knock at the door. He'd planned to start patrolling the coach, and familiarize himself with the latest set of passengers. The majority he would know, as many were repeat travelers. A couple of names were unknown to him when he checked the manifest.

Matthew turned, hoping Esther would be standing there. Sadly, it wasn't her, but one of the other waitresses stood at the door, waiting for his consent for her to enter. He hurried across and opened the door.

"Compliments of the chef," Mary-Ellen said.

Matthew glanced at the selection of delicate pastries prepared for him, along with a mug of coffee. He took the tray from her. "They look delicious," he said.

Mary-Ellen giggled. "Everyone knows you love your food," she said, then hurried off.

It didn't take a genius to know the chef assumed Matthew had something to do with Esther's appointment. Despite what he'd told Esther, the chef was right. He knew she was competent and knew she'd taken over when Henry fell in a heap. Why wouldn't someone like that be given the opportunity to prove herself?

He slumped into his chair and nibbled at the delicious food prepared especially for him. As much as Matthew appreciated it, he didn't have much of an appetite right now. The reason was clear—he missed Esther, and the thought of not being with her was weighing on his mind.

At the end of this trip, they needed to talk.

Chapter

Sixteen

Esther breathed a sigh of relief as the train whistle blew and they began to move. Slowly at first, as they left the platform, then the train gained momentum. She'd done this so many times before, but not with her at the helm.

She'd spent time after supper rearranging staff as required and now ensured each person knew what they needed to do. Esther had never seen them so happy.

Everyone was relaxed. She could tell by the smiles on their faces. With Henry in charge, it was the complete opposite. "Thank you, everyone. If you have any problems, let me know and together we'll work it out."

The applause that broke out surprised Esther, and she fought back tears of joy. As everyone dispersed and went about their business, she noticed Matthew lingering down the narrow corridor. His expression was tentative.

"Matthew," she said tersely, not meaning it to come out that way. "What can I do for you?" She fiddled with the list in her hands.

He took a few slow steps toward her. "I heard the applause and was certain I knew who it was for. I wanted to check for myself." There was no joy in his words, nor was there a smile on his face. This was all-business Matthew. Wasn't that what she wanted? Except it stung. She'd caused the problem by putting a bridge between them. She preferred the real Matthew, not the man she'd forced him to be by her restrictions. "It looks as though it's already going well."

"It is," she said, then stared at the list in her hands. "I'm sorry, but I have things to do."

"I completely understand," Matthew said, then hurried away. Out of the corner of her eye, she noticed he went into the kitchen. She'd heard what the chef had done—it was a nice touch. One Matthew would have appreciated.

"Esther," someone called, and she turned. Did that mean trouble had already occurred? She smiled and stepped toward them. Esther knew this job would be a challenge, but the biggest challenge so far was keeping her distance from the man she'd become far too fond of.

After sorting out the issue, which turned out to be an easy fix, Esther wandered through the lounge area of the Pullman coach. Apart from Mrs. Kilberry, there were few passengers she knew. It wasn't unlike the line she normally worked. What would happen after today? No doubt she would go back to being a waitress. Mr. Steel would not allow a woman to take over the conductor's job permanently.

It was unfair to her mind. They gave Henry the job based on family ties, nothing more, and look at the mess he'd made.

"Miss Walters, Esther," Mrs. Kilberry called as she wandered about the lounge area.

Esther smiled, then sat down next to their star passenger. "Mrs. Kilberry," she said pleasantly. "Are you enjoying the trip so far? Please let me know if there's anything I can do for you."

The older woman reached out and covered her hand. "I heard what that horrid Henry Boswick did to you. Not to mention the other women. I hope they throw away the key," she said indignantly.

Esther was shocked at the woman's words. How did she know? Unless Mr. Steel had told her? "I…I don't feel I should talk about it, Mrs. Kilberry," Esther said. "It's an ongoing investigation."

She stood, but Mrs. Kilberry motioned for her to sit down again. "I never liked him," she said firmly. "Horrid man." Mrs. Kilberry shivered. "Mr. Horton, on the other hand…" She raised her eyebrows, and it took all Esther's efforts not to laugh.

"We are friends," she said instead.

"Only friends?" It was clear the revered passenger did not believe her.

Esther sat back against the comfortable seat and sighed. It wasn't missed. "I'm trying to keep my distance. For this trip at least," she said quietly so only her companion could hear.

"Oh, for goodness' sake," Mrs. Kilberry said flippantly with a flourish of her hand for emphasis. "He's a decent man, and a good catch. What is wrong with you?" She scowled then, and as much as Esther wanted to laugh at the woman's antics, she kept a straight face.

"I have a job to do," she said firmly. "I must go now," she said, then stood. This time she didn't look back, and didn't sit back down to hear the words she already knew—that Matthew Horton was the man for her.

~*~

Esther bustled about, ensuring everything was running smoothly. When luncheon was served, the staff were far more efficient than she'd ever seen them. Knowing they wouldn't be harassed or verbally abused was always an incentive to work harder. "Good job, everyone," she said as they hurried into the dining room ahead of her.

Every worker knew how to do their jobs and to do them well. Esther stood back away from the action and watched from a corner of the room. The passengers were happy, the staff were happy, and she could ask for nothing more.

Once everything died down and food was being consumed, she noticed Matthew standing on the opposite side of the room. How she longed to stand beside him. If she was truthful with herself, Esther really wanted to be held in his arms.

When she glanced across at him for a second time, Esther could see he was miserable. It was totally her fault. These past days they'd spent together were filled with joy. She couldn't have been happier, and it seemed Matthew had been happy too.

Even before the stopover, despite all the drama they'd endured, he seemed more cheerful than he was right now. Esther's heart thudded. It was all her fault he was so disheartened. First she'd led him on, told him she wanted to be with him. Then suddenly she'd rejected his advances, and told him to keep his distance.

Trying to right what was an obvious wrong, she stepped toward him. Would he turn away or leave the dining room completely? On her way there, one passenger stopped Esther. They'd received the wrong meal. "I apologize," she said, meaning every word. "Let me sort this out for you." She hurried past Matthew and into the kitchen, situated not far away. She soon returned with the correct meal, once again apologizing.

The moment she entered the dining room, her heart pounded. Matthew was gone.

Perhaps he was no longer interested—that's exactly what she deserved. She glanced about the room, ensuring everyone was happy and enjoying their meals. Esther then returned to the conductor's office to ensure everything was as it should be.

The heartwarming mood she had on the previous journey was gone. She wondered if it would ever return.

Chapter

Seventeen

Matthew understood Esther had a job to do and knew he was a distraction. The moment she left the dining room, he did too.

So far, this journey was uneventful, which was exactly how he liked it. He wandered around the lounge area, ensuring all the windows were totally uncovered and the area outside was visible. Not that he expected another attempted robbery after the last one was such a failure. They had all but eliminated the Renegade Gang. Levi Hayes was the only surviving member. Those members not killed at the time bled to death, he was told. Hazardous occupation. It might seem harsh, but he had no sympathy for men like that.

Especially when it put those he loved at risk.

Matthew stumbled as he navigated the long corridor on the way back to his office. Since when did he use the *L* word? Besides, he and Esther barely knew each other. They'd done several trips together, including this one, which had only just begun. Was it really only such a short time? It felt like he'd known her forever.

There was a tap at the door, and when Matthew glanced up, the woman of his thoughts was standing there. He motioned for her to enter. If he opened the door to Esther, they'd be standing close together. If he was near to her, he would want to kiss her. This was far safer.

"Take a seat," he said matter-of-factly, as though they were mere acquaintances. "What can I do for you?"

Esther stared at him for far too many heartbeats, and he wondered what she was about to say. "It's Mrs. Kilberry," Esther said firmly. "She says we are meant to be together."

Matthew frowned. "And what did you tell her?"

Esther closed her eyes for several moments before opening them again. "I told her I needed to get back to work."

Matthew couldn't help himself. He laughed out loud. "She's a determined old biddy," he said, then reached across the desk. When his hand covered hers, his heart fluttered. "But she's right. I felt it from the moment we met." He studied Esther—she wasn't denying it.

"I…" She glanced first at their entwined hands, and then at him. "I've missed you," she said quietly.

They sat staring at each other for what seemed like an eternity. Matthew's heart pounded as he waited for her to say more. When she didn't, he spoke up. "I've missed you, too. Far more than I ever imagined possible." He reached across with his other hand, and she offered her free hand. That was a start, at least. "I've never felt like this before, Esther. And that's no lie."

Her eyes sparkled with unshed tears, and he wanted nothing more than to hold her close and never let go. Matthew glanced across at the glass windows and door of his office. "A bit of privacy would be nice," he mumbled. Then he grinned and stood, pulling her along with him.

"The hidden jail cell," Esther said, laughter in her voice. "I love it!"

The moment they were away from prying eyes, he pulled her into an embrace. Esther didn't resist, as he knew she wouldn't.

Her arms went up around his neck, and he leaned down to kiss her lips. Her warmth filled him, and his heart fluttered from the moment their lips met.

He couldn't wait to get back to Timberlake Junction and spend far more time with the woman he loved. "I love you, Esther," he whispered in her ear, and Matthew felt shock run through her.

"I love you, too," she said quietly. Then she chuckled. "Mrs. Kilberry will be pleased," she said, then her lips covered his, and all was right with the world.

Before leaving Matthew's office, Esther sat at his desk for a few minutes. "I need to make it look as though we've been working," she told him.

"No, we don't," he said firmly. "We owe no one an explanation. I'll rest easy now, knowing you don't hate me."

Surprise registered on her face. "I could never hate you, Matthew Horton. Is that what you thought?" Esther glanced down at her lap. "That wasn't my intention. I do, however, need to concentrate on my job. I must prove to Mr. Steel a woman can do this job as well as any man."

Matthew loved her sass. He was looking forward to getting to know her better and seeing her feisty side show.

"What are you thinking about?" Esther asked as she studied him.

He chuckled. "You really don't want to know." Matthew stood then. "Should we visit with Mrs. Kilberry?" He laughed again.

"You wouldn't dare!" Esther said, her exasperation clear.

He opened the door for her and followed her out. "Just watch me," he said, and headed toward the lounge area. "Oh, Mrs. Kilberry," he called, teasing Esther.

He chuckled as she ran in the opposite direction.

Matthew stood next to Esther in the dining room that evening, far from the passengers as they ate. As predicted, all went smoothly. He had never seen a journey that ran so well. The weasel had a lot to answer for.

"I never heard from the marshals," Esther suddenly said, her voice low.

"Turns out Dr. Dunne made a statement on your behalf. You don't need to worry." Matthew pulled her hand behind them and squeezed it gently. "I hope the weasel gets what he deserves," he said.

"You really hate him, don't you?" Esther asked, worry on her face.

Matthew frowned. "You don't? After what he did to you, you're willing to forgive him? Even though you still bear the bruises and pain he caused?" He glanced down at her arm. "You're a far better person than me, Esther Walters. I will never forgive the man for what he did to you and other women. I only wish I'd known."

"Forgiving his sins helps me more than it will ever help Henry. Not forgiving him turns to bitterness and anger. I choose not to live my life that way." Esther's expression told Matthew she wanted him to do the same. "Are you a Christian, Matthew?"

It wasn't a subject he normally talked about. He swallowed as Esther studied him. "I am," he said quietly. "But it doesn't mean I have to let him off the hook. The man is a criminal, and a fool." The moment the words were out of his mouth, Matthew felt guilty. He knew, as a Christian, he should forgive those who wronged him—it was even in the Bible.

He heard Esther sigh and knew she was upset at his words. Suddenly, he pulled her out of the dining room. They didn't really need to be there, anyway. It was a habit he'd gotten into over the years. This way, he checked everyone was where they should be, and nothing untoward was going on. Mrs. Eastlake immediately came to mind, and Matthew wondered how the dear soul was faring in the hospital.

When they arrived in the lounge area of the coach, he indicated for her to sit down. He sat close to her without being too obvious should passengers arrive. "I don't have empathy for Henry Boswick. He harmed far too many women." Matthew ran a hand through his hair. "If only I'd known…" He let his words trail off. It was something he would regret for as long as he lived.

Esther's eyes opened wide. "You can't forgive Henry because you don't forgive yourself," she blurted. She reached across and held both his hands.

He shook his head, then stopped. Her words confused him. Was that really the case? Perhaps Esther was right—he'd never thought about it before now. Matthew frowned. She squeezed his hands. Why did he suddenly feel so emotional? "I don't get to church often," he blurted out. "This job, you know—it's not always easy."

She blinked a couple of times, then stared at him. "A church is merely a building," she whispered. "It's the people who make it special."

Esther was right. Without people, a church was nothing but a building. If you had love in your heart, and you lived by the teachings of Jesus, you were a Christian. The thought sent warmth soaring through him.

"Do you mind if I say a prayer?" Esther asked quietly. Before he had a chance to answer, she clenched his hands. Matthew closed his eyes. "Lord, help us forgive those who have wronged us. Show us a way to let go of the bitterness and hatred before it eats us up inside. In your name, Amen."

"Amen." Matthew felt different. It was strange, but peacefulness seemed to come over him. Was it the words Esther had said, or something else entirely?

They stood together, and he enveloped her. Holding her in his arms felt good, and Matthew knew they were meant to be together for all time.

The low murmurings of the passengers alerted them the meal was over and the hordes were headed their way. Esther stepped out of his arms, and Matthew felt—empty. He knew they had to act professionally while onboard, but he wanted to hold her. Unfortunately, it wasn't possible while they worked.

"Esther, Mr. Horton," Mrs. Kilberry said. Did she catch them in each other's arms? "It was inevitable, you know," she told the pair, then beaming found herself a comfortable seat.

Matthew glanced at Esther, who glanced back at him. Then they both chuckled. It seemed their relationship was no longer a secret, and frankly, Matthew didn't care.

Chapter

Eighteen

It seemed to take forever to arrive back at Timberlake Junction. If she was honest with herself, Esther was dreading it.

She'd enjoyed her time as a conductor for the Pullman coach, even if she had been pulled in several directions. Despite being a complete novice in the position, Esther knew she'd done a far better job than Henry ever had. It sounded vain, she knew, but it was the truth. The staff had been the happiest she'd seen since she'd arrived on this line, and things had gone smoothly.

If past experience meant anything, Mrs. Kilberry would report back to Wallace Steel, owner of the railway. That thought gave her pause. Is that the reason Mrs. Kilberry was on this journey? To assess her ability as a conductor? Her heart pounded, and she forced herself to calm down. Esther knew she'd done an excellent job, and any feedback given to Mr. Steel would surely be positive.

Her future was uncertain, and not knowing where she stood was weighing on Esther's mind. Things could go a few ways—they could transfer her back to her original route. This was, after all, meant to be temporary while Martha recovered.

Poor Martha. With the woman now dead, would they ask her to stay on, or would they find a replacement? Either way, Esther would go back to being a lowly waitress. It was a pity—she had really enjoyed her short stint as a conductor. She was naturally organized, and that skill had been quite useful in carrying out her conductor duties.

A tap on her office window brought Esther out of her musings. Glancing up, she noticed Mrs. Kilberry standing there. It was a rare occurrence indeed. Esther opened the door and ushered the older woman inside.

"Do you have a moment?" Mrs. Kilberry asked, then sat before Esther responded.

Esther would always make time for Mrs. Kilberry. She might be rich and influential, but Mrs. Kilberry had become more like a friend. "Of course. Anything for you, Mrs. Kilberry." Esther pushed a pile of papers into a neat little pile, then waited to hear what the passenger wanted.

"What are your plans for the future?"

If nothing else, Mrs. Kilberry was blunt. Her question stunned Esther, but only momentarily. "My… my plans?" she finally managed to get out. "I don't understand." She was truly confused. Why would the woman sitting in front of her ask such a thing?

"I'm here on behalf of Wallace Steel. I might look like a dithering old woman," she said, trying to hold back a laugh and failing miserably, "but since my husband passed on, I oversee our national corporation. Wallace asked me to assess your skills."

"Assess my…." Esther stammered. She was taken aback by the admission. Esther took a moment to compose herself, fiddled with the already ordered papers, then studied Mrs. Kilberry. "What conclusion did you come to, Mrs. Kilberry?" Her heart beat in her ears, and Esther felt lightheaded as she waited for an answer. She knew she'd done an excellent job, but that meant nothing if the woman in front of her believed otherwise.

Mrs. Kilberry reached for her oversized bag. "I already knew before I was tasked with this assessment you were perfect for this position. Henry Boswick won't be back, no matter the outcome of the investigation." She waved a hand in the air. "The man's a fool. And a bully. His uncle is an even bigger fool for giving him the job to begin with." The older woman sighed, then pulled some papers out of the bag she now held on her lap.

Esther watched her every move. "I ask again," she said, pulling a wad of papers out of the bag. "What are your plans for the future?"

"Apart from working on the railway, I have no specific plans." Esther was confused now. What were the papers, and what was this conversation really about? She opened her mouth to ask when those same papers were pushed toward her.

"This is a contract. Wallace Steel is offering you a permanent position as conductor on this line. He is fully aware it was your doing that the robbery was averted. He also knows what you did to help poor Mrs. Eastlake when she fell. Not to mention you noticed her missing."

It was difficult to take it all in, and Esther's mind was reeling. "I was doing my job," she whispered.

Straightening her back, Mrs. Kilberry studied Esther, then seemed to choose her words carefully. "You were doing Henry's job. He should have noticed those things, but he was far too busy trying to do as little as possible." She pushed the papers even closer to Esther. "This is a contract to secure your services as conductor for the Helena line. Read it over, and when you have done so, and are happy with the conditions, sign it and return to me."

"I honestly don't know what to say," Esther said. "Apart from the fact I know nothing about contracts. How do I know if there's something untoward in it?" At that moment, Esther felt as though there were eyes on her. She glanced up to see Matthew watching her. He was grinning at her, then hurried away. Did he know what was going on?

"My dear girl," Mrs. Kilberry said. "I've already had my lawyer go over the contract and approve of its contents. I won't have you taken advantage of." She paused momentarily. "Shall we go through it together?"

Esther nodded. There was far more to Mrs. Kilberry than she could have guessed. The scared little old lady she met when she first arrived was a ploy. She felt like laughing, but this meeting was far too serious for that.

What would Matthew say when he found out? Or was he already fully aware of the situation? Knowing him, it would be the latter. He usually knew what was happening the moment it occurred. Sometimes, even before.

Esther was still reeling from her earlier meeting with Mrs. Kilberry as she wandered through the lounge area. Mrs. Kilberry sat comfortably, sipping her tea and nibbling on a large cookie. She winked at Esther as if to say, my real identity is between us.

Everything was running smoothly, the staff had been given their tasks, and there was little left for Esther to do.

It was difficult to believe that in less than an hour's time, they would arrive back at Timberlake Junction. When they did, it would be chaos. Ordered chaos with bags being removed from the train, and passengers alighting. Esther would stand at the bottom of the steps and ensure no one was injured coming down. The platform would be all hustle and bustle, and a hive of activity. It was one of the biggest stations in the entire state of Montana.

Esther smiled. How could she go from waitress to conductor in such a short time? She enjoyed her new job and knew she would never tire of it. Especially when it meant she would see more of Matthew Horton.

He was not the demon Henry Boswick made him out to be, and Esther made sure everyone knew it. What a horrid man Henry was. There was no doubt in her mind Mrs. Kilberry had been watching him. Why else would she travel so often?

"Ah, Mr. Horton," Mrs. Kilberry said. "I've not seen much of you this trip." She tipped her head to the side. Esther had come to know she did that when she was curious about something. "When are you going to marry this young woman?"

Esther's mouth dropped open, but Matthew grinned. "I'm not sure she's interested," Matthew told the older woman, then turned to Esther and chuckled. He stepped forward and put an arm around her waist. Esther's heart fluttered at the touch, and she melted against him. She suddenly stood straight, realizing they were in public for all to see.

Mrs. Kilberry beamed. "I want an invitation to the wedding when it happens," she said, then went back to her tea and cookies.

Still reeling from the woman's words, Esther glanced up at Matthew, who seemed shocked, then moved out of his grip. She made her way through the carriage, stopping to speak to each of the passengers. She ensured they were ready to alight when they arrived at Timberlake Junction. Most were seasoned travelers and knew exactly what was required of them.

Returning to her office, she ran into Matthew again. "Esther, wait," he said, as she tried to hurry on. "I have something I want to say."

She glanced up at him. He looked far more serious than she expected. "I have a lot to do, Matthew," she said, trying to dismiss him.

Suddenly, he dropped to one knee, right there in the middle of the train. "Just because Mrs. Kilberry…"

He shook his head and reached into his pocket. "It has nothing to do with her. I've had this burning a hole in my pocket, too afraid to ask." He held out a ring box, then flipped the lid open. The sparkling diamonds caught her eye. Esther gasped. "Esther Walters, will you marry me?" Matthew asked, his voice trembling.

Esther blinked. It was the last thing she'd expected to happen, but her heart was filled with joy. "I will," she said, and Matthew slipped the ring on her finger. He stood and pulled her into his embrace.

"I love you," he whispered in her ear.

Esther rested her head against his chest. "I love you too," she whispered back.

Epilogue

Two years later…

Matthew checked on Esther as often as he could. This would be her last trip as a conductor. As much as he had protested, she insisted on continuing to work. Wallace Steel had allowed it, only because it was Esther. According to the railway owner, she was the best conductor they'd ever had. He'd even presented her with an award, confirming the fact.

Being the first ever female conductor had opened doors for other women. Matthew knew full well if Henry had not behaved so brutally, the opportunity would never have arisen. Now locked safely in a jail cell for his crimes, no one need worry about Henry Boswick again.

The train jolted and Matthew panicked. Was Esther knocked down? He ran toward the direction of her office, hoping she was sitting down and saved from being thrown to the floor. Her office was empty.

He ran frantically about, trying to locate her. It finally hit him—she was likely talking with Mrs. Kilberry. The older woman still rode the train whenever time allowed. She had all but retired from her position as head of her company, allowing her eldest son to take over.

As he entered the lounge area of the Pullman coach, Matthew's breath whooshed out. "There you are," he said, calmness coming back to him. "Are you alright?"

"Of course she's alright," Mrs. Kilberry said. "We've been having a lovely talk. To be honest, I'm not sure what I will do without Esther. I love our little talks, and she is the best conductor this railway has ever had."

Matthew was filled with pride. He knew from the moment they met, Esther was special. He hadn't realized how special she was, but he certainly did now.

Sitting down next to his wife, Matthew felt his heart rate slowing. She told him often he was far too protective, but he knew it was really that she was willing to do whatever was needed. Sometimes it put her in danger.

Esther reached for his hand and put it to her swollen belly. "Baby is doing somersaults," she said as she chuckled. Matthew's heart filled with joy. It wouldn't be long and their baby would arrive—less than two weeks. If he had his way, she wouldn't still be working. "Oh!" Esther said, with what sounded like pain in her voice.

Matthew studied her. Mrs. Kilberry watched her carefully. "Are you alright?" Matthew asked warily. He knew how much Esther hated to come across as weak.

She screwed up her face, and he knew she wasn't. His hand still on her belly, Matthew felt it contract. "Are you in labor?" he asked firmly. "I knew you shouldn't have taken on this last trip," he said, annoyed with himself for allowing it. Not that Esther would have listened if he had forbidden it.

"Perhaps," Esther said, her voice telling him far more than her words did. She stood then, and Matthew stood with her.

He checked his watch. "We still have quite some time before we arrive at Timberlake Junction," he said. "In the meantime, I want you to stay here with Mrs. Kilberry."

The older woman patted the seat where Esther had sat moments earlier. As she moved to sit down, Esther's waters broke. "Oh my Lord," Mrs. Kilberry said. She turned to Matthew. "Is there a doctor on the train?"

His brain was in turmoil, and he couldn't think. Was there a doctor on the train? He pulled the passenger list from his pocket. "Doctor Francis Dunne is traveling with us." Relieved, Matthew hurried to find the doctor.

~*~

"The good news is, first babies usually take their time. We should arrive at Timberlake Junction well before this baby arrives," Doctor Dunne said. "It is far better to have your baby away from the train with all its jolts and jerks."

Matthew squeezed Esther's hand. "Thank you, Doctor," he said. "You are always here when we need you."

"I travel a lot to present lectures," he said. "It's pure luck I was here. My lecture was canceled at the last minute, so I'm returning earlier than expected."

"I'm so glad you are," Matthew said. It was then Esther screamed.

Doctor Dunne examined her again. "My goodness," he said, concern now showing on his face. "This baby is ready to come into the world. How long have you been having pains, Esther?" He studied her, his face stern. "All day, I'm guessing," he said without waiting for an answer.

"Perhaps," she said, as Esther often did when she was not prepared to tell the entire story.

Doctor Dunne turned to Mrs. Kilberry, who had suggested they transfer Esther to her room. "I'm glad we took up your offer, Mrs. Kilberry," he said. "How do you feel about assisting me with a delivery?"

Matthew was stunned. "Delivery?" he asked. "We will be on solid ground in less than..." He checked his pocket watch. "An hour."

"This baby is not waiting." Doctor Dunne opened his medical bag. "Have the chef boil some water—and plenty of it. That's a good man," he told Matthew, who was still trying to take it all in.

He hurried to the kitchen and returned a short time later with two large bowls of boiled water. Right now, Matthew was very grateful for the kitchen trolleys Esther often used before she became a conductor.

"Thank you, Matthew. Now I need you to leave," Doctor Dunne said firmly. "Mrs. Kilberry and I have this in hand, and will let you know when the baby arrives."

He was pushed out of the room before he knew what was going on. Still stunned, Matthew returned to his office but couldn't sit still. Then he went to the kitchen and made a cup of coffee. Chef took him to the staff's break room and sat him down, handing Matthew a small plate of pastries.

He stared down at them—he wasn't hungry, but with Chef's urging, he took a bite. His stomach wasn't cooperating, and he gave up after a while. "You can eat them later," Chef said before he left Matthew alone.

Matthew wasn't one to wallow, but right now it's how he felt. His wife's life was at stake. Never did he believe their baby would decide to come early and arrive while they were still on the train.

Sipping his coffee, Matthew did the only thing he could— absolutely nothing. This late in the trip, there was nothing for him to do. Mary-Ellen, one of the waitresses, sat with him. While he appreciated the company, neither could do anything to help Esther. Or the baby.

They could only sit and wait.

What seemed like forever later, but in truth, was less than an hour, Mrs. Kilberry found Matthew. Mary-Ellen was still with him, and they both stood.

"You have a son," Mrs. Kilberry said excitedly. "Esther is in perfect condition, and so is your boy. All thanks to Doctor Dunne." She was beaming, and suddenly stepped forward and hugged Matthew. "Congratulations," she said. When she stepped back, Matthew noticed her tears. Mrs. Kilberry had become more of a friend than a passenger.

Mary-Ellen squealed, then hurried away. Likely to inform the rest of the staff.

Matthew hurried to where he'd left Esther. She lay quietly on the bed, her eyes closed. The baby was in her arms. "Thank you, Doctor Dunne," Matthew said. "I don't know what we would have done if you hadn't been here." Matthew heard the emotion in his own voice.

"Congratulations," the doctor said, apparently not wanting to even think about that scenario.

Matthew went to Esther's side. He leaned in and kissed her forehead, then stared into the face of their son. "Thank you for this gift from Heaven," he said. Two years ago, he hadn't envisaged he would be a father now. He was a lonely man going through the paces.

Esther made his life worthwhile, and now they were a family. He sat on the side of the bed and silently prayed. Giving thanks to God for bringing Esther into his life was something he did regularly. Today, he also thanked him for the safe delivery of their baby boy. If they were blessed with more children, he would do so each time.

As he stared down into the baby's face, he could see Esther staring back at him. He loved this woman with all his heart and knew they would spend the rest of their lives and eternity together. Along with as many children as God deemed they should have.

From the

Author

Thank you so much for reading my book – I hope you enjoyed it.

I would greatly appreciate you leaving a review where you purchased, even if it is only a one-liner. It helps to have my books more visible!

Multi-published, award-winning and bestselling author Cheryl Wright, former secretary, debt collector, account manager, writing coach, and shopping tour hostess, loves reading.

She writes both historical and contemporary western romance, as well as romantic suspense.

She lives in Melbourne, Australia, and is married with two adult children and has six grandchildren. When she's not writing, she can be found in her craft room making greeting cards.

Website: *http://www.cheryl-wright.com/*

Facebook Reader Group:
https://www.facebook.com/groups/cherylwrightaut hor/

Join My Newsletter:

https://cheryl-wright.com/newsletter/
(and receive a free book)